JULIE
Sanctuary Series

CW00529954

By
Michelle Dups

Michelle Dups
2023
x

<u>DEDICATIONS</u>

This book is dedicated to my group of St. Anne's mum's. You know who you are. Thank you for your unfailing support, encouragement, and meals out.

Long may our traditions and friendships continue.

You ladies rock!

LIST OF CHARACTERS

Macgregor Brothers – Leopard Shifters

Dex – Mated to Reggie – Twins Boys – Ben & James

Falcon

Jett

Duke

Zane

Reggie's Foster Sisters

Jaq, April, Elle

Russo Brothers – Hyena Shifters

Anton

Luca

Landry Siblings – Wild Dog Shifters

Joel – Mated to Julie

Amy – Mated to Rory & Sean Whyte

Jack – Landry Father

Rose – Landry Mother

Julie's Sister

Hannah

Moore Sisters – Elephant – Non-Shifters (CURSED)

Renee

Lottie – Mated to Kyle Whyte

Ava – Twin to Marie

Marie – Twin to Ava

Whyte Family – Multi Shifter Family but mainly Gorilla

Annie – Mother – Gorilla Shifter

John – Father to Kyle (Human) - DECEASED

Kyle (UNABLE TO SHIFT SHOWS SHIFTER TRAITS) – Mated to Lottie Moore

Rory – Twin to Sean - Gorilla Shifter (adopted son of Annie) – Mated to Amy Landry

Sean - Twin to Rory – Gorilla Shifter (adopted son of Annie) – Mated to Amy Landry

JULIE

CHAPTER 1

I was driving the hour to the Landry's coffee farm as a favour for Annie, she had asked me to take a basket of jams and sauces to Joel who was Amy's brother. Amy was mated to Annie's sons Sean and Rory. I wasn't sure why they couldn't wait for Amy to take them with her when she came back from town at the end of the week. Annie had been insistent that I take them.

I had met Kyle, Annie's youngest son, when he'd come to the hospital with his mate Lottie who had been attacked by her father. They had been accompanied by one of the best doctors in the area, Jett MacGregor. When I had let slip that my family wanted to force me into a mating, they hadn't been happy and had insisted that I leave with them and go with Lottie to help with her recovery. I hadn't wanted to say *'no'* as Annie and her family had done so much for me the last five months that I had been hiding out with them from my biological family.

The last five months have been the best of my life. Annie and her sons had adopted me into their family, and I now had a family that loved me unconditionally, something that I had never had before. Lottie and Kyle had just found out that they were having twin girls and I couldn't wait to be an aunt.

I thought Jett may have been upset with me when I had decided not to go with him to their ranch to be the onsite nurse. Instead, the Whytes had built a clinic on their farm and I now was the nurse for both the Landry's and the Whyte's as their farms shared a border. Jett said this worked out better and it had been decided that each farm or ranch would build a clinic and have them fully stocked that way. Jett and I didn't have to carry anything with us. So far it was working well.

I found it strange that in all the months that I had been with Annie and the boys, I hadn't met Joel. We seemed to keep missing each other. To be fair though, I hadn't made it to any of the gatherings except one at *'The Lake'* and, on that occasion, Joel had stayed on the farm as they had issues with a shipment of their coffee so he had to cancel.

My biological family had been quiet in the last month and I hoped that they had given up looking for me. They had questioned all the main ranches and farms in the area, but I don't think they realised what a tight-knit group this was that lived here. From what I understood when they had met at the Russo's, they annoyed them so much that Anton had threatened to shoot them if they ever stepped foot on their ranch again. Hearing about that had made me laugh when I had met them at the last gathering. I loved the closeness the families had.

As I drove along I took in the sights around me. Since I had never been to Amy and Joel's farm before, I was making sure to take note of all the landmarks that had been placed on the map that I was given. I had passed the turnoff to the house that Sean, Amy and Rory were building so I knew that I had about another thirty minutes before I reached the farm.

I saw the coffee tree's up ahead, I knew that I was close, slowing down. I turned left and went under a hanging sign that stated I was now on *'Landry Coffee'*. I drove over a cattle grid that had shaken my entire car. I wondered why they had it as they didn't have any cattle on their farm.

I could see buildings glowing white in the distance, as I drove down the road. Changing down a gear, I made my way up a steep hill towards the buildings. There were acres of coffee trees on both sides of the road. I seemed to drive forever before the road levelled out and I passed what must have been the workshops and factory. I could smell the coffee so I wondered if they were roasting the beans. Amy had told me not only did they sell and grind their own coffee, they also roasted and exported the beans.

I left the workshops and factory behind me and continued down the road to where I hoped the house was. I drove through an avenue of trees, I could see just up ahead, the entrance to the main house. Driving through the entrance, I took in the garden that was looking sorely neglected. The grass was dead and the flower beds were full of weeds.

Since there didn't seem to be any designated parking, I pulled the car under a tree. I got out of the car and took in the house ahead of me. It must have been a beauty in its day, but now it had a sad and neglected air. The house had a beautiful high pitched faded green roof with scalloped eaves.

Dirty concrete steps that went from wide at the bottom and narrowed at the top, leading up to the veranda that was enclosed by ornate wrought iron. Looking around the veranda there wasn't a single piece of furniture to sit on. It was barren. The white paint was peeling off the walls. The saving grace was the gorgeous double wooden doors that had beautiful stained-glass panels on either side.

Walking up the stairs I got a closer look at the images on the glass and saw that the animals showcased were leopards, wild dogs, elephants, and hyenas. These were the animals of the four main families. Surrounding the animals were flame lilies and ferns as well as waterfalls. Whoever had done this had been extremely talented. I could see where Amy got her creativeness from.

I knocked on the door and waited, but nobody came. That was strange since I knew there was usually always someone in the main house.

Taking a chance, I pushed on the handle of the door and it opened under my hand.

Walking in, I called out "Hello, anyone home?"

There was a range of faded scents in the house, and I could tell no one was home from the lack of noise. Thinking I would find the kitchen and leave the box there, I ventured further into the house. To my right was an arch that led to a large lounge area. There were large couches that had seen better days. Everywhere I looked there was a thick layer of dust coating the exposed surfaces. If I didn't know better, I would have thought that nobody lived here anymore.

Carrying on further into the house, I passed a dining room with a table big enough to fit about fifteen people. I knew Amy came from a big family, but I hadn't realised it had been that big.

Finally, I made it to the kitchen. I could see signs of life here with the number of dirty plates in the sink as well as the coffee spilt on the cupboard and floor. The only saving grace was that the trash bin seemed to have been emptied. After taking everything in, I wondered if Amy realised how much her brother was struggling

Placing the box in my arms on the sticky table, I went to the sink and pulled all the dirty dishes out of it so that I could wash them.

Four hours later, I had done every room in the house except the bedrooms. I hadn't ventured into them. I'd found all the cleaning supplies in the laundry room and hadn't been surprised at the amount of laundry that had piled up, I decided I might as well do the laundry too since I was cleaning.

Now that the house looked better, I sat down at the newly cleaned kitchen table and realised I was starving.

Calling Annie, I waited for her to pick up the phone.

"Hi baby girl, everything okay?"

It always filled me with a warm feeling whenever she called me baby girl.

"Hi Annie, I just wanted to let you know what I found when I got here and to let you know not to expect me back until late."

"What's wrong? Is someone hurt?"

I bit my lip and thought before I replied. I didn't want to overstep, but I could see how much Joel was struggling and wasn't sure if Amy was aware.

"Annie, I'm not sure if Amy knows or not but I think Joel is struggling. There was no one in the house when I got here so I tried the door, it opened so I came in. I know how everyone is with each other so I didn't think it would be a problem. I was just going to set the box in the kitchen and leave, but Annie the house was a mess. I don't think it's been cleaned for months. The gardens, including the vegetable garden out back, are in a bad state. I've cleaned the house except for the bedrooms. And I think that I will cook a meal before I leave. I'm not sure where Joel or any of the workers are because I haven't seen anyone since I arrived."

I heard Annie sigh on the other end of the phone. "The last time I saw Joel, I did wonder if everything was okay. Amy has been so busy getting the new house ready for her, Sean, and Rory, and doing all the books that I don't think she has been up to the house for months now. Do you want me to come over and help?"

"No, I will be fine Annie, I just hope he's not mad finding me in the house, adding in the fact that I've cleaned it."

"Oh honey, I'm sure he won't mind and will be thankful. Is there food in the house?"

"Yeah, the fridges and freezers are full. I will see what I can find in the garden vegetable wise."

"Okay baby girl, call if you need any of us to come over."

"I will Annie, thank you. See you later tonight."

After saying goodbye to Annie, I made my way over to the veggie garden to see if there was anything salvageable from there for supper tonight.

Heading back into the house I decided to make a couple of meals that could be frozen. I had managed to find enough vegetables to make soup, and I thought I would make stew, chicken and dumplings and for tonight a lasagne as the pasta in the pantry would be expiring soon.

It looked like a busy afternoon for me, but as I love cooking, it wasn't a hardship.

Finding some music on my phone I put it on and got started.

JOEL

CHAPTER 2

I had been working so hard the last couple of months without a break. I didn't want to let my sister Amy know how much I was struggling. She was newly mated and busy with the books for our farm and the combined business we had with the other four families. I knew she had also taken on doing most of the book-keeping work for her mates' family.

The problem was our farm had gone from being run by four people full time to just me doing full time and Amy part-time now that she was mated. I knew that if my parents and Amy could see how I had let the house and gardens go they wouldn't be happy. Part of the reason was that our housekeeper had left unexpectedly on a family emergency and wouldn't be coming back, that was three months ago. I was short-staffed but didn't have enough time to hire new staff.

I was slowly drowning, and the only good thing was the finances. I was exhausted from working from five in the morning until sometimes eight or nine at night. All I had time to do was throw some food in my stomach and head to bed. The last time I had seen any of the other families was probably about four months ago. I had been having Amy go to the meetings as she knew all the financial side of our family business. I knew that I was going to have to say something soon as I couldn't keep on like this. I couldn't remember when I had the time to change and spend time in my Wild Dog form. That's how tired I was. It didn't help that every time I saw one of the Whyte's my animal went a little nuts because they always smelt like cinnamon sugar, which affected me for some reason. It had gotten so bad that I was limiting my time spent with them.

Taking one of the motorbikes from the workshop because I didn't have the energy to walk up to the house. Looking at the time I saw it was 5 p.m, all of us had left the factory on time.

Arriving at the house I recognised the vehicle parked there as one of the Whyte's, taking a deep breath I let it out as a sigh, wondering who it was and hoping it wasn't Amy. I hoped it was Annie or Kyle as I would find it easier to talk to them.

Getting off the bike I made my way slowly up the stairs taking in the neglected air of the house and feeling ashamed that I had let it get this bad.

Quietly opening the front door, I walked in and stopped in surprise, the hallway floor was gleaming. It was so clean, poking my head into the sitting room. I saw that this too had been cleaned. The whole house smelled of lemon and bleach. Underneath the clean smell, there was a faint hint of the cinnamon sugar smell I now associated with the Whyte's, my animal had perked up inside of me. I thought it must be Annie in the kitchen. Taking off my dirty boots I left them by the door and made my way to the kitchen. Amazing smells were coming from there and my stomach was rumbling, I couldn't remember the last time I had had a good meal.

Stopping in the kitchen door I watched the beauty that was dancing around my kitchen to the music coming from her phone. I wondered if this was the elusive Julie that everyone had been talking about.

Her hips moving to the beat, her long nearly white hair with black stripes threading through it was in a french braid that ended just above those lusciously swaying hips. Looking around I took in the gleaming kitchen with containers of cooked food set out on the counters cooling. Set out on the table was a vase with fresh flowers and a salad.

My attention wandered back to the female standing in front of the stove, my cock had perked up considerably and suddenly I wasn't nearly so tired, taking a deep breath I sniffed the air, and my nose was full of the elusive cinnamon sugar scent that had been driving me mad for months.

"Are you going to stand in the doorway all night staring or are you going to say something?" The beauty in front of me enquired huskily, turning away from the stove.

Looking at me with stunning purple-blue eyes framed by the darkest lashes with slight freckles doting over her nose and cheeks. I felt my breath hitch in my chest at the uncertain look on her face. She was biting her bottom lip causing me to groan wishing I was the one sinking my teeth into those plump pink lips.

I slowly approached her trying to get control of my animal, he was doing yips and circles in my head.

Lifting my hand to her cheek I tilted her head up slightly, hearing her breathing hitch as I gently pulled her lip from between her teeth.

"Julie, my elusive cinnamon sugar."

Lowering my head, I feathered soft kisses across the freckles that dotted her cheeks, stopping at the corner of her mouth where I pressed a soft kiss. Running my tongue along her lower lip soothing it from where it had been held between her teeth, her lips were slightly parted, her breath mixing with mine. Leaving her mouth, I made my way across her jaw and towards her throat. Running my nose along her bare neck, inhaling deeply her cinnamon sugar smell until I got to the curve between her shoulder and neck. Pushing her tank top strap to the side I lay kisses along her shoulder before making my way back up her neck. Nipping her gently, I felt her shudder gently against me and the arms that had snaked around my waist tighten. By the time I made it back to her beautiful lips, she was panting slightly, pressing and rubbing against my hard cock causing me to groan in need. Hearing a slight whimper from her, I lifted my mouth to look into her eyes that were hot with need, her pupils dark with desire.

Pressing my forehead against hers I tried to control my need, taking a deep breath I groaned as the smell of her need met my nose.

"Julie," I breathed. "We need to slow down."

"Joel, we really don't. I need you, I'm not sure what is happening, but I feel like I'm on fire."

Picking her up, I set her on the counter and stepped between her open thighs, ran my hands up her thighs under her skirt until I reached the edge of her panties. Running my finger along the edge of the band, she groaned pulling on the back of my hair while she hungrily attacked my mouth. Slipping a finger under the edge of her panties, my fingers brushed against her hot slit finding it dripping wet. Causing her to whimper in need and rock against my hand.

I was unable to ignore her need, I had known the pull of your mate was instantaneous but had not expected it to feel like this. It was like a fire burning through me and only taking her would quench it.

Lifting her I took her to the table and lay her down, pulling her tank down over her shoulder and releasing her breasts I feasted on them, sucking and nipping them into hard points, listening to Julie's whimpers and pleading only fed my hunger for her and the need to take care of her. Pulling her clothing off as I made my way down her body, removing her panties along with her skirt until she lay completely naked in front of me. Parting her thighs, I saw the moisture coating her thighs, making me moan as I ran my tongue up the inside of her thighs until I got to her hot pussy. Running my tongue around the edge of her hard clit caused her to cry out as another gush of her need coated my fingers as I eased them into her. I could feel her pussy pulsing around my fingers, and I knew she wasn't far from another orgasm but this time I knew I needed to feel her around me as she came.

Pulling my shirt over my head and pushing my shorts down, I looked up to see her watching me, her eyes huge in her face, running her tongue over her lips, she pulled her legs up until her heels were on the table and let her legs fall apart.

"Joel," she whimpered. "Hurry."

"I'm here, Sugar." I groaned as I pushed my way gently into her swollen folds. When I could go no further, I stopped panting slightly, bending and resting my head on her chest as we adjusted. I felt her fingers feathering through my hair as I gritted my teeth against the need to pound into her.

Slowly she began to rock her hips against mine, lifting my head from her chest, I looked into her eyes as we found our rhythm and I slowly pushed in and out of her, looking down between us I moaned at the sight of her wetness coating my cock. I could feel the head of my cock start to swell and I knew I was preparing to knot us together and felt bad that I hadn't had time to warn her. I sped up my thrusts and until I was so swollen inside her that I couldn't move, I heard Julie cry out and another gush of wetness covered us as her pussy pulsed around us. Throwing back my head I came hard, lowering down until I was again resting with my head on her chest. Looking up I saw that Julie's eyes were shut.

"Julie? Sugar, open those baby blues for me." I breathed. Growing concerned I ran my hand over her cheek. Just when I was wondering if my mate was ever going to wake up, I heard a deep rumbling purr coming from within her chest.

Making me chuckle slightly at the irony of fate as it seemed my mate was of the feline variety. My animal was going slightly nuts and he wasn't very happy with me for not marking her as ours yet. I rolled my eyes and told him to be patient. We had all night.

Feeling Julie, nuzzling at my hand where it lay against her cheek. Lifting my head from where I had laid it back down on her chest, the rumbling of her purr a comfort under my cheek.

She was watching me from under lowered lashes, her cheeks flushed. I groaned slightly as she moved her hips. Gripping them tightly in my hands as I held her still.

"Don't move baby, it's going to take a little while for me to soften and I don't want to cause you any pain," I apologised.

"Joel," she whispered, "I still need." One of her hands was plucking at her breast and the other was making her way down to her clit, she was still whimpering in need, brushing her hand away from her clit, I gently circled and rubbed until she was writhing on the table her legs wrapped firmly around my hips. As I pinched her clit she lit up and wailed long and low as she came, another gush of wetness covered us. Until finally she lay still and sated on the table.

Gently pulling her up into my arms, I picked her up and carried her with me still locked inside her to the shower. I could feel myself finally softening. We had just entered the shower and I sat down on the ledge built on the side to get the water going when I felt her animal waken and groaned as she bit down hard into my shoulder marking me as hers. Panting slightly my head against her shoulder I didn't even try to fight my animal as he made himself known he struck her just between her shoulder and neck where everyone would be able to see her mark.

We stayed sitting like that until I slowly slipped from her body causing her to whimper softly.

"I know, Sugar," I gently pressed a kiss to her temple, holding her close to me. Moving us into the warm water I washed my mate, who seemed too slowly to be more coherent.

Feeling her hands running through my hair as I knelt to wash her legs, I looked up with her eyes soft in her face, she whispered smiling at me, "I wasn't expecting you, Joel." There was happiness radiating from her face.

Grinning up at her I replied, "Or me you, but I'm not complaining."

JULIE

CHAPTER 3

Looking down at the handsomely grinning face on the male knelt at my feet, I couldn't help but think about Jett telling me that one day I would understand what it meant to have a mate that put you first.

My legs still shaking from the orgasms he had wrung from me. I sat back down on the ledge with a giggle.

Cupping my face in his hands I looked up into eyes that were exactly like Amy's. His eyes at the moment were filled with concern. "You okay Sugar?"

Smiling up at him I replied, "I'm good honey, just got shaky legs that's all and I'm suddenly starving."

Switching off the water he got out and went to grab clean towels from the cupboard by the door. I watched the muscles play in his back as he reached up, he wasn't as bulky as my brothers or the MacGregors, but he was still well-muscled, and I knew he was strong as he had picked me up and carried me around like it was nothing.

Watching him walk back to me, his cock hanging long and thick down the inside of his legs. I moaned at the sight and squirmed slightly on the bench in the shower at the sight. Catching his eyes as I lifted my eyes to his face, to find him smirking at me.

"Let me feed you first before we go there again," he grinned at me while he wrapped a towel around his waist.

Helping me up he wrapped the second towel around me and picked me up, took me to his room and set me on the bed while he went to the walk in to get clothes. Looking around I saw that this must be the master bedroom and while it needed redecorating it was a decent size with full-length windows covered with net curtains down the one side. Taking a closer look, I saw that one set was doors and if open you would be able to walk straight into a courtyard that had a fountain in the middle. Getting up to take a closer look, I opened the doors and stepped out onto a narrow veranda, looking around I saw that several doors were leading out onto the veranda. Making my way to the fountain, to have a look around I could imagine how beautiful this would be if it was running and surrounded by flowers and ferns.

"Julie," I heard Joel call from the doorway.

Returning to him I saw that he had found me some sweatpants and a t-shirt of his to wear.

Slipping the shirt over my head I pulled it on and found it a bit tight in the chest but otherwise, it fit okay. I went to take the pants and found him holding them out for me to put on. Stepping into them, I looked up at him as he pulled them up over my hips.

"Do you think this is strange?" I questioned.

He looked puzzled, "Is what strange?"

"The fact that I jumped you as soon as you came into the kitchen and that it feels like I have known you all my life?"

He laughed and pulled me into a tight hug, "No, it's the way of mates. I feel sorry for humans as they don't know straight away like we do that we have met our soul mates."

Thinking it over, I decided he was right and this was much easier. Nodding, I agreed, "Huh, you are right this is much easier. Although I have to let Annie know as she is expecting me back tonight."

"Okay, but after we have eaten," he agreed.

He grabbed my hand and pulled me from the bedroom back down the passage to the kitchen.

I blushed scarlet at seeing our clothes lying around the kitchen and grabbed up the anti-bacterial spray and started wiping down the table and counters.

Hearing him chuckle, I saw he was collecting our clothes and taking them through to the laundry room.

Going to the stove I pulled out the lasagne and garlic bread I had put in the warmer earlier and brought it to the table.

Joel had already laid the table, I noticed we were sitting on the bench seat by the wall. Not that I minded, I needed to be close to him.

"Beer, soft drink or water," he asked, turning from the fridge to look at me.

"Water," I replied sitting at the table and started to dish up our supper. Looking at the clock I saw it was nearly seven o'clock in the evening.

My phone rang just as Joel sat down next to me. Grabbing it I saw that it was Annie and knew I couldn't ignore it.

"Hi Annie, I'm sorry I didn't call earlier," I answered.

"That's okay baby girl, I just wanted to make sure you are okay and if Joel made it home yet?"

I smiled, thrilled at hearing the concern in her voice. I don't think my biological mother had ever been concerned about me.

"I'm good Annie. Joel is here with me, and we are just eating supper." I confirmed. I hesitated, I felt Joel's hand on my leg and looked up as he gave my knee a small squeeze in support.

"I won't be coming home tonight, Annie," I whispered shyly.

We heard Annie let out a squeal on the other end of the phone and heard the others in the background asking her what was going on.

"Hold on, sweetie, I'm going somewhere more private away from your nosy brothers."

Over the phone, I heard the back door open as Annie walked away from my brothers. Feeling a tap on my lip I looked up to see Joel holding a loaded fork to my lips, opening my mouth I took a bite. The flavours burst over my tongue causing me to moan. Joel's eyes grew hot as he watched me lick my lips.

"You and Joel better not be doing anything while on the phone with me young lady," commented Annie.

"I would never Annie," I spluttered, laughing.

Joel must have heard what Annie said because he was laughing too. He continued to feed me as Annie, and I chatted while she made her way outside.

"Hmmm, okay. Right, I'm outside away from your brothers and their nosy mates. Tell me, are you happy?"

Smiling, I answered, "So happy Annie."

There was a sniffle from the phone, "That's good, baby girl. I will miss having you at home, but I couldn't be more blessed in the mates my children have chosen."

My eyes welled with tears, "Oh Annie," I wept.

Joel took the phone from me and pulled me into his arms, dropping a kiss to my head, "Annie, there is no need to be sad. You will always have a room here if you need it, I will never take Julie from you."

"Oh Joel, honey I know, ignore me, I'm just a little sad that I only just got a daughter and now she is moving out. I am thrilled for you and Julie. Can you get away with her and come over tomorrow?"

"Of course, we can, I will make the time. I will look after her, Annie," confirmed Joel.

"I know honey, I couldn't wish for a better mate for her. Now let me say goodnight to my girl and I will see you tomorrow."

Taking the phone back from Joel, I listened to what Annie had to say about tomorrow and then said goodbye. Drying my eyes on the bottom of my shirt, when I finished, I took a deep breath and looked at Joel who was looking at me with soft eyes.

"Tell me about Annie and your brothers? I know a little but not a lot as I haven't been to any of the meetings recently. I only know that we are to look out for strangers."

"Okay," I answered. "But I will need the chocolate cake I made earlier if I'm going to talk to you about my biological family."

Joel got up and grabbed the cake from under the net on the counter and came back with a fork for us to share, making me smile.

Pulling me back under his arm I snuggled into him, trying to think of the best way to explain my family.

He stroked down my arm and twinned his fingers into my hand, "Start anywhere, Sugar, it doesn't have to be at the beginning."

Taking a deep breath, I let it out slowly, "My earliest memory is from when I was about two and must have got out from the nursery and my mother was shouting at me, of course, I had no idea what she was shouting about, anyway my nanny came and took me back to the nursery. I don't think I saw my parents again until I was about six, by then I had four younger siblings, they all looked completely different to me."

"I think it was about the time I realised that I looked different to my family. They all looked related with red hair, shot through with black highlights and brown eyes, whereas I looked like this.

"Anyway, over the years I was hidden away, and the others were paraded out. I come from a wealthy family and as far as they were concerned, I tainted their bloodline. We were all home-schooled, and I went years without seeing my parents.

"Once we no longer had a nanny it got harder because we no longer had meals delivered to the nursery. My siblings were allowed at the dinner table, but I was not in case someone saw me. The servants tried to sneak me food but if they got caught, they got fired. I got used to eating sparingly or hiding food. My youngest sister Hannah used to sneak me food until she was caught, I told her I was not worth the punishment she got. She was beaten so badly and lost so much blood that I was worried she wouldn't make it. She's the only one of my family that I consider worth keeping in touch with, we have a way of communicating in code so that they don't find out. I hate to think what they would do to her if they found out.

"Mostly I kept my head down and kept away from the family. When I was eighteen my old nanny came to visit me and brought a letter from the solicitors. My grandmother on my mother's side had given it to her before she died. She had left me some money that nobody knew about. It was enough for me to go to college and become a nurse. That night I packed up my bags and left. I haven't been back since. Just before Lottie, Kyle and Jett came to the hospital my father contacted me to tell me that he had found a mate for me. This male already had cubs and didn't want any more so there was no chance of my tainted blood being passed on."

Joel was growling next to me, and his hand was squeezing mine, I could see his canines just under his top lip. Running my hand through his hair soothingly, I stayed quiet until he had calmed down enough for me to continue.

"I was going to go ahead with it as I had always wanted a family and I knew I could love the cubs. That was until I saw how Lottie and Kyle were in the hospital, I knew then that I didn't want a forced mating. Jett and Kyle found out and made it easy for me to leave the hospital and come hide out here. They adopted me into their family unit not long after that and I have had the best five months of my life since I have lived with them." I hesitated and then whispered, "Until now."

Joel pulled me onto his lap and buried his head into my neck taking deep calming breaths until he had calmed down enough to talk. All during the telling of my story his animal had been growling and there were grooves in the table from where his nails had bitten into it.

"I'm sorry, Sugar, nobody should be made to feel like they are not enough. You will always be enough for me and when we have pups or cubs, they will know they are loved. Even when we were struggling financially my parents always made sure we knew we were loved and wanted. And you never have to go hungry again," he promised.

Holding his cheeks in my hands I looked into his eyes, "I know honey and I'm okay now, I promise. But we do have to talk about my family and why they want me back. I need to speak to Jett first as he has been digging up information."

Joel nodded, "Okay we can contact him tomorrow when we get to Annie's. For now, let us forget about everything and take this cake to the bedroom with us, I feel like we haven't done it justice."

Agreeing with him, I got the milk out of the fridge and followed him to the bedroom to enjoy our cake and worry about my biological family tomorrow.

JOEL

CHAPTER 4

I woke up early the next morning before the sun had even risen, yet I felt more rested than I had for months, and I knew that it had to do with the female that was currently nestled in my arms.

Her smell had been haunting me for months and I couldn't understand how I hadn't made the connections. I knew what my mother would say, *'Things happen when they should, how they should at the time they should. Rushing never works.'* She was always imparting little words of wisdom during our childhood. I needed to call them today to let them know about Julie.

Deciding against waking Julie as we had been up most of the night, I slid gently out of bed, chuckling softly at her grumbling as she pulled my pillow towards her and buried her face in it and settled back to sleep, I gently pulled the covers over her and tucked them around her to stop the cool morning air from waking her.

I made my way to the bathroom to shower and get my day started. After showering, I headed to the kitchen to see what I could make for breakfast. Seeing all the meals that Julie had made me were still out I filled the freezer with them and took out some bacon and sausage. There were still some eggs leftover from yesterday's collection, but first, coffee was needed.

Once the coffee was done, I took my cup out to the front veranda and sat on the steps. I needed to see Rory about replacing the furniture that my parents had taken with them when they left. For now, the step would do, I watched the sun slowly rise and with it, the day became nosier as the birds and roosters woke up and started crowing. I was just finishing my coffee and was contemplating getting another one when I heard Julie's footsteps coming towards me. Feeling her brush her lips on the crown of my head, her cinnamon sugar scent filling my nose, tilting my head up I accepted the kiss she left on my lips.

"Morning honey," she hummed huskily against my lips.

Before handing me one of the cups she had with her. Making her way down the stairs she moved my legs and sat between my legs on the step below me. Letting out a sigh of contentment as she leaned back against me to sip her coffee. Pressing my lips to her temple I wrapped my free arm around her chest and held her to me.

"Morning, Sugar," I replied.

Not wanting to rush, just enjoying the morning before we had to get moving and back to our daily lives.

Julie sighed as she finished off her coffee. Tilting her head back to look at me with her gorgeous eyes. "I guess we need to get going huh?"

Hugging her tight, "Yeah, but it will be a good day. Let's get some breakfast and then I can speak to the farm foreman and the factory manager to let them know I won't be here today. They can still contact me if they need to at Annie's. Amy should be here today anyway to do the books and we have no shipments going out this week. So, it will be an easy day."

"Okay," she replied, standing and grabbing the cups to go inside. Grabbing her hand as she was about to walk away I stood, pulling her against me and kissed her, it started slow and sweet and ended with us pulling away panting. Groaning, I buried my head into the crook of her neck where my mark was. Pressing my lips to it, I reluctantly pulled away knowing that if I didn't, we wouldn't be leaving here today and I didn't put it past my sister and her mates to come looking for us.

Grabbing her hand, I tugged her behind me to the kitchen, I muttered under my breath that, "Maybe cooking breakfast would stop me from wanting to ravish my mate at every turn."

Hearing a laugh from behind me, I looked over my shoulder at my mate who was looking at me with laughing eyes. My breath hitched at her beauty.

"Cooking isn't going to stop me from wanting to ravish you," she declared, chortling with laughter as we entered the kitchen.

Making me grin.

We settled into an easy rhythm of getting breakfast ready and on the table. Once we were done, she sent me off to see my staff as she cleaned up. I was surprised at how quickly we had become in sync with each other. I made a mental note to take her to see the clinic we had built for her. I was glad Lottie had brought it up in the last meeting. It made sense to have a fully equipped clinic on each property so that Julie and Jett didn't have to carry equipment around with them.

Jumping on the off-road bike I rode down to the factory to leave instructions on what was needed for today and where I would be if I was needed. Once that was done I arranged for one of the drivers to take Julie's vehicle back to the Whyte's so we could travel together.

I got into one of the farm 4 x 4's and went to pick Julie up so we could make our way to her family.

I knew today would be hard for her, leaving Annie's where she had been safe and loved the last few months but I would do everything I could to make sure she knew she was wanted and valued.

JULIE

CHAPTER 5

Hearing Joel pull up outside, I went out onto the veranda to meet him. I was sad that I was leaving Annie's but also happy that I had found my mate. I now understood what Amy and Lottie had been telling me for months. It was a feeling like no other when you met the other half of your soul. It felt like all those blank empty spaces that you didn't even know you had, were filled up.

When I got to the veranda, I saw that the vehicle I had arrived in yesterday was pulling out of the yard with one of Joel's drivers. Pulling the front door closed, I made my way down the front steps just as Joel was getting out of the vehicle he had arrived in.

Opening the passenger door for me, he picked me up bridal style and deposited me in the passenger seat. I grinned at him and leaned forward to brush a quick kiss on his jaw.

"Thanks, honey," I said, smiling at him.

He looked at me, his brown eyes soft, shining bright back at me with happiness. His face now relaxed from all the strain that had surrounded him last night when he first entered the kitchen.

"Anytime, Julie," he replied before shutting the door and making his way around to the driver's side.

We spent the hour it would take to Annie's, chatting and getting to know each other. Joel told me about what it was like growing up with so many siblings. Wild Dog shifters tended to have multiples, Joel and Amy were twins.

He explained how hard it had been on his parents and how it had caused tension when money was tight. He went on to explain that the families weren't like they were now, where everyone chipped in to help when it was needed.

His parents hadn't had a big support system. Amy and he had helped a lot with their younger siblings and he knew it had affected Amy. He was worried about Amy and her reluctance to have pups.

He had noticed when Annie had told them about the Moore family when they were last together at *"The Lake"*, that there was tension between Sean, Rory and her.

He hoped she spoke to them soon and explained her fears. He had tried to explain to her that it wouldn't be the same as when their parents had pups. Everyone would help, plus she had two mates, not just one.

Annie would help too, and he knew their parents would visit more often if there were grandchildren.

I had noticed that there had been some tension recently, especially as Lottie's pregnancy progressed. Add in the fact that Amy had disappeared for about a week last month on a business trip and hadn't taken either of her mates, instead she had gone with Ava, Marie, and Renee Moore. I knew my brothers hadn't been happy at having their mate four hours away with no way to get to her quickly if they were needed. Luckily, Renee had called to speak to Lottie every night and had given them updates. I had a feeling their business week coincided with Amy being in heat, because when she came back, she was pale and looked drawn.

"Was Amy in heat that week?" I queried Joel.

He sighed and nodded, not looking happy. "Yeah, I tried to dissuade her from going, originally she was going to go alone, but Renee was here the day we were arguing and suggested that she and the twins go with Amy. That way if she needed anything, they would be there to help. They booked a hotel and Amy spent the whole week in the room until her fertile had passed. It wasn't a fun week for her, I promise."

"I know," I replied. "She does know there are other ways to prevent having pups."

Joel heaved another sigh and replied, "She knows, but that would mean she would have to talk about why she is reluctant to have pups. And Amy is great at burying her head in the sand and hoping the problem will go away while pretending all is fine. I just hope that Sean and Rory are patient enough to wait her out."

Picking his hand up from where it lay on my thigh, I placed a kiss on his knuckles.

"I know they are, but if the worst comes to the worst they can always just torture her gently until she does talk to them." I laughed out loud at the look of horror on Joel's face.

He shuddered. "Thanks, I don't need that in my head. It's bad enough that I had to hear them when they stayed over before their house was ready."

He paused, then winked at me. "Nice to know you aren't opposed to being tied up though."

I felt my face heat up as I blushed scarlet, I wasn't sure if it was embarrassment or if it was because I was turned on at the thought of Joel tying me up.

I heard a groan and turned to look at him from under lowered lashes.

"Babe, you need to stop thinking whatever you are thinking, I can't turn up at Annie's with a hard-on," he muttered, adjusting the front of his shorts with a grimace.

I sniggered at his predicament. He turned slowly and looked at me with raised eyebrows. "Not sure why you're laughing, missy. You know they will be able to smell that you're turned on."

I was horrified when I realised he was right. "Quick tell me about your other siblings and no more sexy talk from you until after we are on our way home tonight," I grumbled, making him laugh.

That is how we spent the rest of the trip to Annie's, with him telling me about all the scrapes his younger siblings managed to get themselves into. He kept me laughing at their antics until we drove through the gate at the main house.

On the veranda was my entire family waiting on us, I couldn't stop the smile that spread across my face at my three brothers standing with arms folded across their chests, waiting on the bottom step.

Joel hadn't even stopped the car before I jumped out, hearing his alarmed shout behind me, "Julie, what the hell?"

I ran up to my brothers and tackled them, causing them to fall to the ground and we ended up in a happy pile, laughing.

"Julie!" I heard snapped from behind me.

"Oh, oh, you're in trouble," sang Kyle laughing at me.

Turning, I looked at Joel who was scowling at me.

He wasn't very happy with me.

"I swear to God, woman, I am going to paddle your ass. What the hell? You don't just jump out of a moving vehicle," he yelled as he gently pulled me up off my brothers and into his arms.

Returning his embrace, I instantly felt bad because I could feel how hard his heart was beating and I could smell the fear clinging to his skin.

Soothingly, I ran my hand through his hair. "I'm sorry, Joel. I didn't think how it would look to you. I'm a large cat so I always land on my feet. I was just so happy to see them standing there, trying to look all big, bad, and threatening, when I know they are happy that it's you I mated with."

I felt Joel take a deep breath as he tried to calm down.

"Don't ever frighten me like that again. I'm not sure that I can take anything happening to you."

I nodded. "Okay, honey, I'm sorry." I leaned up and laid a soft kiss on his cheek.

Annie came down the stairs, laying a soft hand on Joel's shoulder.

"Welcome to the family, Joel," said Annie, wrapping her arms around him in a tight hug before turning to me, and pulling me into her arms.

"So happy for you, baby girl," she beamed, smiling at me, before passing me along to each of my brothers who hugged the stuffing out of me.

"At least it's someone we like," grinned Rory, clapping Joel on his back as he made his way back up the stairs. I followed him up until I got to Amy and Lottie who were waiting for me at the top of the stairs.

"Yessss," squealed Amy, jumping up and down before grabbing me in a hug. "I'm so happy it's you. I would have hated it if I didn't like his mate."

Her exuberance made us laugh.

Lottie was beaming at me with happiness. "I'm so happy, Julie. I can't wait to tell Jett. He thought you were meant for one of his brothers."

There was a growling behind me as Joel pulled me into his arms.

"Mine!" he snarled.

There was a look of surprise on Lottie and Amy's faces, they had never seen Joel like this. He was usually the easiest going out of all the males.

Amy snorted at him and patted him on his chest. "Relax, we know. Nobody is going to take her from you. That doesn't mean I can't tease Jett that we are all mated and they are falling behind," she said, grinning mischievously.

I had been so involved in our conversation, that I hadn't even realised Annie and Kyle had left until they came back out onto the veranda with a tray piled high with sandwiches and drinks for all of us. We all sat down to enjoy an early lunch and catch up before I had to pack up all my things to take to Joel's.

I got comfortable on one of the couches next to Joel, leaning against his side after pulling his arm over my shoulders and laying my head on his chest, while listening to the conversation he was having with Rory regarding replacing the furniture on our veranda. I made a mental note to ask Annie for some plants to take back with me as the garden at Joel's place was bare.

I became aware that everyone had fallen silent and was watching us.

"What?" I questioned.

Amy and Lottie started laughing.

"You may not be a Whyte by birth, but you have certainly picked up their habit of arranging mate's to your satisfaction," laughed Lottie.

I felt my face flush. We were always making fun of Kyle, Rory, and Sean for arranging Lottie and Amy to their satisfaction when they sat down.

I peeked up at Joel through my lashes. "Sorry. Are you comfortable like this?" I motioned to the way I had situated us.

Joel smiled down at me. "It's all good, Sugar."

Turning back to my sisters-in-law, I shrugged my shoulders as I looked at them.

"See, it's all good," I said, all smiles.

There were snorts of laughter from Amy and Lottie, but my brothers just nodded in approval.

After lunch, Annie and I went to pack up my bedroom while Joel went with my brothers to see the clinic and what would be needed at our place to get it ready for me and to pick out some furniture for the veranda.

Joel had asked me if I wanted to help choose but I told him that Rory's work was so good that whatever he picked I would love.

JOEL

CHAPTER 6

I nearly had heart failure when Julie jumped out of the truck while it was still moving. I should have realised that she would be fine, it didn't stop me from worrying though. I pulled her away from her brothers into my arms for my own sanity.

After I was welcomed into the family, I couldn't help but wonder why I had stayed away for so long. My sister had been mated to Rory and Sean for months and, in all that time, I hadn't been over to visit.

After lunch, Julie went with Annie to pack up her belongings. I could tell that the two of them were struggling with Julie leaving. I would ensure that Annie knew she always had a place at ours.

I went with Kyle, Rory, and Sean to check out the clinic that they had built for Julie. We had started on ours but I wanted to make sure that I had everything as it should be. Having stocked clinics on each farm or ranch was going to make a huge difference to Jett's workload.

Once we had seen the clinic, they took me to have a look at the furniture that Rory had in storage.

"I don't have much stock right now as I have a full container shipping out tomorrow for one of the photographic safari camps. But you are welcome to whatever is left," said Rory over his shoulder as he unlocked and opened the double doors to his workshop. I was amazed at the furniture he had stocked and ready to be shipped.

I saw Kyle shaking his head in amusement at my look of amazement as I took in the furniture. I wasn't sure what Rory thought wasn't much because there was still a heap of furniture.

Walking over to what was left, we picked through until I had a three-seater, a two-seater, and three single pieces all made from locally treated wood. There was also a small coffee table that we added and Sean went further into the workshop and found a few end tables that weren't perfect but would be fine for the veranda. All that was needed was cushions, but I would leave that to Julie as I hadn't a clue where to start with them.

Rubbing my hands over the pieces, I took in the amazing details on the carvings of different fauna and flora local to our area.

"Shit, Rory, these are fucking amazing. No wonder you have a waiting list," I exclaimed. "Let Amy know the cost and she can arrange payment for you from the farm accounts."

There was a rumble from the three males in front of me, looking up I saw they were all looking pissed.

"You're not fucking paying for this," growled Sean. "You are family and family doesn't fucking pay for the shit we make."

I was stunned. I hadn't expected such generosity and would have been perfectly willing to pay.

Kyle looked at me and said, "All the payment we need is that you look after our sister, keep her safe, keep her happy, and love her. Nothing else is needed."

I tilted my chin at them in acknowledgement and smiled. "That definitely won't be a hardship. Talking about safety, do you have any information on what is happening with her family?"

Rory shrugged and sighed. "Jett hasn't heard anything new and that is what has me worried. I don't think they've given up. Jett believes they were selling Julie off as the family has run through all their inheritance and the male they had chosen is stinking rich. From the little we know, we have managed to find out he is not a good male and has gone through three wives so far, all dying in unusual circumstances. My worry is for the children that they have left behind. Luca did some recon the last time he went to the city and, so far, they seem to be safe. They are generally left with a nanny and the father doesn't have much to do with them."

A growl rose from my chest at the thought of innocent children being in danger as well as my mate.

Kyle clapped me on the shoulder. "Don't worry too much, Joel. We are all here and those that can shift are running all the perimeters along your borders. The Chief is also aware and has decided to include in their training to run around the perimeter of their village closest to you. You will need to up security closer to the house though."

"Sean and I will come over tomorrow and set up additional cameras we have left over from when we upgraded security here. You will need to add a security gate at the bottom of your road that should be manned 24/7. Hopefully, that will deter them from coming through that way," explained Rory.

I nodded in agreement. "That would be great thanks. I appreciate the help, and if you see or have seen any other security weaknesses just let me know so I can get it upgraded. I don't have your experience so anything you recommend I'll do. There is nothing more important than keeping Julie safe. She has a theory on why her family wants her back and it will be interesting to know if it's the same as Jett's."

We loaded what furniture we could into my vehicle while trying to leave enough room for Julie's suitcases. Then we went back to the main house so I could pick up my mate.

Sean and Rory would bring the rest of the furniture out when they came and check the security that we would need.

JULIE

CHAPTER 7

Packing up my room was bittersweet for me. I had been the happiest that I had ever been in my life in the five short months I had lived with Annie.

Annie had followed me to help pack my things and so we could spend more time together before I left. Packing wouldn't take long as I didn't have much. I only had the two suitcases I'd arrived with and a box full of books that Annie had got for me when she went to town. She said she knew how much I enjoyed reading and wanted to get me a simple gift, I didn't consider it simple at all. I'd never had anyone do something like that for me.

"You know you can visit me anytime, Annie. In fact, if I thought I could get away with it, I'd have you move in with us," I said.

Pulling me into a hug, she murmured, "Ah, my sweet girl, I will be over so much you will be sick of me and Joel will be moaning about his mother-in-law being an interfering pain in the arse," she laughed.

Holding on tight, I tearfully said, "You could never be a pain in the arse, Annie. Thank you for taking me in and loving me. This family is the best thing that has ever happened to me."

"I think you were what our family was missing, Julie. Never forget we are only a phone call away if you need us. Although I have a feeling your brothers will all be over tomorrow checking on security and making changes to keep you safe."

Letting go of Annie, I dried my face with the palms of my hands and met her gaze. Her eyes were red rimmed from tears.

Taking a shaky breath, I slowly released it before smiling at Annie.

"Maybe you could come with them tomorrow and bring some plants with you," I stated, grinning at her. "The garden is in an awful state."

Smiling back at me, Annie replied, "Well then, that settles it, I will see you tomorrow. Can't have you not have any veggies now, can I."

My heart was feeling much lighter now that I knew I would see some of my family tomorrow. We left the room with my suitcases and took them to the veranda to wait for the males to come back.

JOEL

CHAPTER 8

Driving back up to the house, I saw that Julie had finished packing and my heart hurt when I saw that all she had was two suitcases and a box.

Jumping out and walking up the veranda steps, I saw that both her and Annie had red-rimmed eyes.

Pulling them into my arms, I said, "Please don't cry, you two. You are both breaking my heart. Annie, I want you to know you're welcome any time. In fact, you can move in if you want." This made them laugh for some reason.

"Don't worry, Joel. Mum is coming over tomorrow to help with the garden. Ignore us, we'll be fine," Julie sniffled into my shirt.

"Okay then. Are you ready to go, Julie?" I asked.

She nods, "Yep, all packed up and ready to go."

Leaving her with her mum, I grab her bags and add them to the vehicle.

After hugging Annie goodbye one more time and helping Julie into the vehicle, we were off and on our way, back to the farm.

Seeing that Julie still looked a little sad, I pulled her over to me and brought her hand up for a kiss before laying it on my thigh. She smiled at me as she lay her head on my shoulder, her eyes slowly drifted close as she fell asleep.

I was thinking of all the security improvements that I would need to make to ensure that she was safe. It was hard to imagine the type of family she had been born into where they would want to harm one of their children.

Just then my phone rang and the screen showed *"Parental Unit"*. I grinned. I guess Amy had told them about Julie.

"Hello, ma," I answered.

"Hello ma, that's all I get from you?" my mother shouts at me. I can hear my dad in the background telling her to "Calm down before you blow a blood vessel."

I sniggered at the two of them. They were always like this and to people who didn't know them it seemed like they were always fighting.

"Don't tell me to calm down, you old dog, when my son can't be bothered to tell me he has mated."

"Maybe he would tell you if you shut up long enough to let him get a word in," I heard my dad retort.

I was trying to keep my laughter to a minimum so that I didn't wake Julie up.

In the background, I heard my mum grumbling at my dad and then a door slammed. I waited out the muttering from my mum until she finally took a breath.

"Ma, I wanted to tell you I'm mated," I choked out, laughing at her as she sucked in a breath. I waited for the explosion I knew was coming in three, two, one.

"Aagh, you are so frustrating. Just like your father. I know you are mated because I had to find out second hand from your sister in America. Joy knows about your mating and I don't? I'm hurt, Joel. So hurt that you couldn't tell your mother first. I can understand you leaving your father out, but me? Who carried you for six months, kicking me from the inside out and then having to push your big head out? I can't believe I was the last to know." She finally took a breath. "So who is she and is she lovely?"

With my mother, you had to let her run her course and not interrupt her until she got it all out. She alway brought up the fact that she was pregnant with us for six months. Personally, I thought six months was better than the nine months human women had to endure. Although we couldn't help but needle her sometimes.

"You mean you don't know who she is? I'm shocked, Ma, that your gossip line seems to have let you down," I said chuckling at her.

She gasped in outrage. "I don't listen to gossip, you little shit. I merely listen and try to get all the facts before passing them on to the relevant parties."

I finally stopped laughing long enough to take pity on her and tell her about Julie.

"Ma, her name is Julie and she is beautiful both inside and out. She is a Tiger Shifter and is the adopted daughter of Annie Whyte. I thought Amy would have told you as her brothers are Sean and Rory. I hope you and dad can make a trip back to the farm in the next couple of months to meet her."

I heard my mother sniffle at the other end of the phone. "I'm so happy for you, son. You and Amy deserve all the happiness after what we had to put you through helping with all the kids. Amy hasn't called in a couple of months. Joy found out about your mate from Lottie when she called to speak to Amy about something."

I sighed thinking about my sister. "Ma, I think you and Dad need to come out sooner rather than later. Not just to meet Julie, but also because Amy is struggling at the moment about having pups and it's affecting her relationship with her mates. And don't you dare tell her I told you that!"

My mother sniffed at me. "I'm not a gossip about my children, Joel. I can keep secrets you know. But I figured something was going on. Your sister does like burying her head in the sand."

While we had been chatting, I had heard my father come out onto the deck at our family holiday home by the coast.

"Hello, son. Now that your mother is finished giving you a hard time, I wanted to say congratulations. I hear we need to make a trip out. Can you give us about six weeks to sort out the shop here and we will be out?"

"Dad, are you working again? I thought you were retired now," I said grinning.

"Son, you know I can't stay home with your mother, she would kill me," he stated, laughing.

"Too right," I heard my mother say.

"I started a small shop selling our coffee and it's now making a nice profit. Let me hire a manager and get them trained and we will come out."

"Sounds good, Dad. I miss having you and Ma at the farm."

"We miss you too, son. Now that you and Amy are mated, you will probably see more of us. Your mother won't be able to stay away, especially when you start having pups," he said.

"Dad, you and Ma know that you didn't have to leave right?" I spoke.

"We know, son. But after all the years of work you put in, we felt like you needed it more than us. After all, you're the ones that have made it a success. You and your sister have done far more with the farm than I ever did. We're so proud of you both. I know I had to depend on both of you too much when you were young. I laid a lot of responsibility at your feet but you two handled it well. You deserve the farm and I know you will make it grow. We're happy to be here by the coast, but that's not to say we don't miss you all."

I was slightly choked up by my dad telling me he was proud of me.

"Love you, Dad," I said.

"Love you, son. We'll be with you in six weeks, if not before. We will definitely be there in time for Christmas. Here's your mother," he replied, signing off.

"Hey, Ma."

"Love you, son, I can't wait to see you all soon. Let me know if you want us to bring anything with us from here before we come."

"I will, Ma. I'm looking forward to seeing you too. Love you and I will call again soon. We're just coming up to the house now," I replied.

"Okay, son. Look after yourselves and I'll talk to you soon. I'm going to harass your sister now and let her know we will see them at Christmas," she replied, chuckling as she hung up.

The veranda lights were glowing against the darkness of the night as I pulled up to the house. Smiling, I ran my hand gently against Julie's cheek to wake her up.

Wrinkling her nose at me, she grumbled and snuggled in further. Giving up, I laid her gently on the seat of the car and stepped out of the Land Cruiser.

After unlocking the house, I collected my sleeping mate from the vehicle and carried her to our bedroom. Tucking her into bed, she didn't stir once, other to moan that she was tired.

Going back outside, I looked up at the stars shining bright in the night sky and, for the first time in a long time, I felt at peace.

I took Julie's bags to our room, but decided to leave the rest for the morning. Stripping, I climbed into bed with my mate and pulled her close to me, breathing in her unique sugar-cinnamon scent as sleep took me.

JULIE

CHAPTER 9

The weeks following my leaving Annie's home were busy. Between Annie and me, we managed to get the gardens sorted and replanted. I had spoken with Joel's parents and they would be visiting us within the next month or so. With their arrival imminent, we had re-done some of the rooms so that they could have their wing on the other side of the house. This would allow us all some privacy. We would still share the kitchen and living room but I didn't think they would mind. Plus, I was excited to share a meal with them. That was one thing I missed from Annie's, our big family dinners.

My clinic was finished and we were just waiting for it to be stocked. Jett would be bringing all the items I needed when he next came over. For now, I was commuting between our farm and Annie's place. It was the best of both worlds for me since I got to see my family often and Joel and I ended up always staying one night a week with them.

My brothers had come over and upgraded our security systems and spoken to the guards. All the staff were made aware not to allow strangers onto the property. I never left without at least one other person in the vehicle with me. I was having to use back roads so that it was less likely for someone to see me, but this was making the journey longer. I hated that my birth family were causing so many issues. I was hoping that Jett had found out some more information so that I could finally have some peace and that they would just back off. After years of ignoring me they were suddenly all up in my business. I didn't want anything to do with them except for my youngest sister and I was starting to get concerned about Hannah.

We had a way of leaving messages through social media and I hadn't heard from her in nearly two months. This was very unusual for her, especially considering the longest we had gone with no contact was three weeks. We left messages in code and there had been no warning in her last message other than her father seemed to be on a rampage and she was looking forward to going back to college and getting out of the house. My last three attempted contacts were showing as unread.

When I'd mentioned it to Joel, he'd contacted Jett and they were looking for her, but so far they hadn't found her. She hadn't turned up at college on enrolment day. To make matters worse they were having to do it all on the sly so that my family weren't tipped off.

Joel had been trying to keep my mind off it all and I was keeping as busy as I could. The next family meeting was to be at our home so that I didn't have to leave the sanctuary of the farm.

The rest of my life seemed like a fairy tale to me. I had never expected to find someone like Joel or the way my life was filled with love and family like it was now. I was looking forward to meeting Anton and Luca Russo as I had not yet met them.

At the present moment, I was busy baking and prepping food for the meeting tomorrow. I knew everyone would bring something with them but the need to feed and care for people was ingrained in me and I was at my happiest feeding people. I knew none of it would be wasted since shifters tended to eat a lot.

I was standing at the sink washing apples for the apple crumble I planned to make, when I felt the heat from Joel's body surround me. His hard chest pressed against my back, his lower half flush against my backside, telling me exactly how he felt about me. I couldn't help but wiggle against him pushing up against his hardness. Joel emitted a low growl that caused my body to shudder at the promise of being filled by him.

His big hands settled on my hips, his fingers flexing as I tilt my head back to look into my mates' heated eyes.

"Mmm, Sugar. I love seeing you in our kitchen. It brings back good memories of our first night," Joel groaned in my ear before laying a trail of kisses down the side of my neck and along my jaw, making me bite my lip to hold my lusty moan at bay.

Turning to face him, I lifted my arms to encircle his neck and pulled his face towards mine, but I stopped the motion when our lips a breath away. "I can't get enough of you, Joel," I whisper before I seal my lips to his. That was the truth whenever he was near, I ached for him, the need to touch him overwhelming me until I had no choice but to give in. There was not a thing I could do about the ache, until I physically touched him. A big part of me knew it was my tiger yearning to mark him as ours, but for me, it was the feeling of safety and love that Joel gave me from having him close.

As our kiss lingers Joel's hands began to slide from my hips, down my thighs, his fingertips feathering over my skin leaving a trail of goosebumps in their wake. My breath hitched in my throat as his large hands tunnelled under my skirt. Each of his palms grabbing handfuls of my backside, his fingers flexing as he pulls me tighter to him. My tiger purred at his possessiveness, I let out a loud whimper as he circled his hips, grinding his hard cock against my stomach. Lifting one of my legs I hooked it around his waist, opening myself up to where I need him the most. His cock bumps against my clit and I moan, rocking my hips and rubbing up against his impressive length, causing Joel to rumble low in his chest. The sound ramping up my excitement, the friction we were creating was hitting the right spot as I chased my impending climax that was rushing up on me so fast, I couldn't stop it, the coil tightened and tightened before it snapped.

"JOEL," I moaned long and loud as my climax bursts free.

Panting slightly, I lay my head against his shoulder as I try to control my breathing. Joel's hips still slowly rocking against me drawing out the last remnants of my orgasm.

Feeling his hardness pushing against me. Frenzied my hands hurry to the button on his shorts, my fingers shaking from the need to please my mate. In my haste I rip his shorts open sending the button scattering across the kitchen floor.

Joel's eyes burn into me as I drop to my knees in front of him, my mouth watering at his scent. Seeing him swollen and throbbing in front of me, with precum leaking from the head of his cock.

My pussy clenches hard, reigniting the flames of my excitement, I tense my thighs, rubbing them together hoping that it would ease the ache that Joel has stoked at the mere sight of his perfect cock. Sticking out my tongue I flatten it against the root of his cock and drag it slowly up his length. Glancing upwards, I see that Joel's head is hanging down, his eyes closed, and his breathes are coming hard and fast, his lips are parted, and as I engulf him in my mouth, his lips kick up in a smile. I moaned as his flavour burst over my tongue causing my eyes to close.

Opening my eyes, I gazed upwards again this time to find his animal staring down at me. His face was tight with tension, his eyes lowered, and I knew he was fighting his control to not cum down my throat, though I wished he would. Joel reaches for the hem of his shirt and yanks it over his head, dropping it on the floor, his muscular chest now bared to my gaze I moan as my clit throbs with need.

Joel's biceps contract as his hands work to gather my hair from my face, wrapping it in around his fist, keeping his grip gentle. Taking him deeper, I swallowed, making him groan, long and loud into the room, his hands clenching in my hair as he loses the control he was fighting and begins to slowly rock into my mouth, bumping the back of my throat. His eyes heat as his jaw ticks as he starts to pull away, but I sink my nails into the hard globes of his arse halting his retreat, my tiger growls at the thought of my mate removing himself from our mouth.

"Sugar, I'm going to cum," he muttered, his face tight from holding back.

Refusing to let him go, I feel my claws come out as I hold on to him tighter, with my eyes locked on his I make my intent clear and continue to draw his cock deeper into my throat as I clenched my muscles around his cock Joel growls and shouts out my name as his body grows tight, shuddering as his release shoots from his cock and into my mouth.

Swallowing, I take all that he gives me until he's spent, I lick his cock clean, smiling to myself that I was able to make him lose control. Breathing hard, Joel drops to his knees in front of me on the floor. My cat feeling slightly smug at seeing our mate sated and kneeling naked on the floor before us. Pulling me into him he takes us to the floor, his back on the cool tiles holding me to his chest, that is rising and falling as he tries to catch his breath.

He was perfect, and I loved to look at him.

Pushing up so I could look down at my mate I grinned down at him. "Did you come in for something in particular?" I asked.

I bounced slightly on his chest as he laughed.

"I came in to tell you that everything is set up outside for tomorrow and to ask if you wanted to go for a run with me? Although, I'm not complaining about what just happened. I now think the kitchen is my favourite room in the house at this point," he grinned up at me.

I snorted with laughter as I tucked my head into his shoulder. We lay like that for a little bit, his hand slowly drifting through my hair, my chest rumbling with a purr with every stroke.

He gently nudged me. "So do you want to go for a run?"

Sitting up, I straddled him, running my hands over his chest as I looked down at him.

I loved looking at him. He was much more relaxed now that we were mated and not as stressed. I knew he was looking forward to having his parents here over Christmas. We hadn't replaced the housekeeper yet since I was managing for the moment, but I knew I was likely to get busy now that the clinic was finished and would need help before long. But that was a worry for another day, for today I would go for a run with my mate and, tomorrow, I would welcome all our family into our home and hopefully find out what was going on with my biological family.

Jumping up, I reached down and pulled Joel up from the floor.

"I would love to go for a run with you. Can we stop at the hot springs?" I asked while pulling my clothes off and throwing them on the laundry room floor.

Turning around when I didn't receive an answer, I saw Joel watching me with heated eyes.

"Oh no," I said, backing away laughing. "You promised me a run."

"Are you sure you want to go for a run," asked Joel, licking his lips, his cock hardening as his gaze swept me from top to bottom.

I pushed the door open, staying just out of his arm range because I knew that if he got his hands on me I would cave and he would then go for a perimeter run later without me, which would make my cat very unhappy.

I shouted over my shoulder, "The last one to the springs does laundry this week." Then allowed my tiger to take over from me as I took off at a run. Hearing a growl from behind me, I looked back and saw my mate chasing me. I knew he wouldn't catch me but my cat loved the chase.

I was still smiling when he finally caught up to me sitting naked in the hot springs waiting for him.

Smirking at him, I asked, "What took you so long."

I squealed in laughter as he pounced on me and dug his fingers into my ribs tickling me.

"What took me so long," he rumbled, making me shiver. "I had to check the perimeter, not just make a straight run for the springs. I can't believe my mate is a cheat," he muttered as pulled me onto his lap.

I finally stopped laughing and lay my head on his shoulder with a deep sigh of happiness.

Looking up at the stars in the night sky, I couldn't believe how much my life had changed in such a few short months.

Tilting my head back on his shoulder, I looked up at Joel, taking in his smiling dark eyes, his dark hair slicked back against his head. Pressing a kiss to his throat, I sighed with happiness.

"I love you, Joel."

Joel pressed a kiss to my temple, his arms tightening around me.

"Love you too, Sugar."

JOEL

CHAPTER 10

The contentment I felt was hard to explain as I laid with my head back on the rock behind me enjoying the heat of the hot spring with my mate snug in my arms.

Gone was the bone-weary tiredness that had plagued me the last couple of months. It was like I had been sleepwalking until the day I had found this beautiful female in my kitchen. She amazed me every day with her kindness and compassion. She had taken over running the house, the clinic, and sorting out the gardens with ease.

I knew she hated having to travel with someone with her for security, but she never complained.

Not only had she slipped effortlessly into my life, but my mother was also shouting her praises from the rooftop and couldn't wait to meet her. Julie had taken it upon herself to phone my parents to find out when they would be arriving and if they had any particular meals that were their favourites. She was looking forward to having them come stay and had worked hard making sure the suite that we had readied for them on the other side of the house, was done just right. She had also phoned all my siblings and made sure they knew that if they wanted to come home for any reason they would be welcome. I had a message from each of them on how lovely my mate was and that I had better not do anything to fuck it up, which amused me no end.

I was taking a leaf out of Kyle and Dex's book and making sure that she knew without a doubt that she would always come first in my life.

Her breathing started to deepen and I knew she was starting to fall asleep.

Nudging her gently, I tilted her head up and gazed into eyes that were hazy with sleep.

"Sugar, let's get you home and into bed," I said, standing her up in the pool.

"Why," she grumbled. "I was comfortable."

One thing I had found since our mating, Julie hated to have her sleep interrupted.

Getting out of the hot spring, I leaned over to offer her my hands to help her out.

Once she was out, I pulled her naked body against mine and ran my hands up and down her back, waiting for her to wake up a bit more before we allowed our animals to take over.

"Okay," she said, pressing a kiss to my chest. "I'm awake, let's go home."

I waited for her to shift into her tiger, taking the time to admire her strength and size in this form. Her coat glowed a gorgeous white in the moonlight. She chuffed at me and rubbed her head against my side. I knew she was wondering what was taking me so long.

Letting my Wild Dog out, I shifted and suddenly my hearing and vision was so much clearer than when in human form. Nudging my mate with my head she took off for home. I followed along behind her.

In the distance I could hear the Chief's guards running along the perimeter border where our property met theirs. I was thankful that they were happy to help with security.

I knew the chief had a soft spot for the women in our families. After hearing the history of what had happened between the Moore family and the Chiefs family, I could understand it.

Up ahead Julie stopped, waiting for me to catch up. Side by side we walked together, our animals comfortable with each other until we reached home.

JULIE

CHAPTER 11

I was so relaxed after our run and swim in the hot springs, that after a quick shared dinner with Joel, I fell straight into a deep sleep and didn't stir until the next morning. Rolling over, I saw that the bed next to me was empty. Looking at the time on the clock, it showed five a.m. I knew that Joel would already be at the factory getting the work for the day sorted.

Jumping out of bed, I headed to the shower to get ready for the day. I was looking forward to seeing everyone and getting to meet the Russo's since I hadn't met them yet. Finishing my shower, I dressed in a summer dress in blue with big white flowers printed on it. The dress hit just above my knees. I needed to stay cool with how busy I was going to be, because today was set to be another hot day.

Entering the kitchen, I saw that Joel had left the coffee pot on and my cup was sitting ready for me. Next to the cup was a small bouquet of mixed blue and red salvia with a note attached, *'Thinking of you, xxx'.* Smiling, I added the note to the tin on the shelf to join the other random notes I found during the course of my day that Joel left me. Pouring my coffee, I picked up the flowers and put them in the vase sitting on the table already filled with water.

Grabbing the apple crumbles that I had prepared yesterday from the fridge, I put them in the oven. The meat was marinating, and I had been told not to worry about salads as the Moore's sisters would bring that. Annie was providing the bread. Balancing my coffee in one hand, I picked up the tray with the tablecloths and cutlery on it to take outside with me. I was glad that Joel had already set up the tables on the veranda yesterday, that made everything so much easier.

Dropping it all off on the table, I took my coffee and sat down on the top step to watch the sunrise over hills. This was my favourite time of day. I loved how the day slowly came alive. The birds had just started singing, the automatic sprinklers had come on to water the garden and the water drops were glistening in the rising sun. From the workshops and factory I could hear the staff shouting greetings to each other. In the distance I could see the loaded truck leave the factory to go into the city with a delivery of coffee.

As I sat there I counted my blessings. My life had changed so much in the last few months. All for the better.

Finishing my coffee, I got up and went to cook breakfast as I knew Joel would be coming back to the house soon and I was starving. All the families were scheduled to arrive around eleven o'clock and lunch wouldn't be served until around one o'clock. *'Full English breakfast was what I felt like this morning,'* I thought as I got all the ingredients out of the fridge.

I was just starting on the eggs when I heard voices in the hallway. It seemed that my brothers had arrived early. Rolling my eyes, I went to get more bacon and sausage out of the fridge to cook as I knew they would want to be fed.

"Mmm, that smells amazing," I heard Rory say as he came through the doorway.

I grinned up at him as he dropped a kiss on my head and went to the coffee pot to pour a cup.

He was closely followed by Sean and Kyle. They each dropped a kiss on my cheek as they went past me to get to the coffee.

"Morning, little sis," Kyle rumbled, giving me a hug as well.

"Morning," I replied while smacking his hand that was reaching for the bacon on the plate next to the stove.

"Stop trying to pinch the food, you know that never ends well." I grinned at him.

"But I want a snack, I'm fading away." He faked pouts at me, his blue eyes twinkling with laughter.

There were snorts from Rory and Sean.

"Don't believe him, Julie. He was eating a bacon and sausage sandwich when we picked him up," grumbled Sean from where he was sitting at the table.

"Hey, I'm a growing boy, I need my protein," laughed Kyle as he helped himself to coffee and joined our brothers at the table.

Rory had got extra plates and cutlery and was laying them on the table.

"Not that I don't love seeing you, but what are you doing here so early?" I asked them.

"We thought we would come and see if you two needed help setting up for today," answered Kyle.

"I think we are good to go," I replied.

Turning away from the stove, I said, "The barbeques may need filling with coal but other than that the food and drinks are organised."

I saw that Rory and Sean were chuckling softly and Kyle was looking slightly disgruntled.

"What did you do, Kyle?"

Rory laughed as he explained that the real reason they were here so early was that Kyle had got kicked out the house because he was driving Lottie nuts hovering over her.

"All I said was that I didn't think she should be saddling a horse while she was pregnant," he griped.

I snorted at him. "You do realise that women have been having babies for centuries, right? And Lottie isn't just any woman, she's half shifter, so she is stronger and heals quicker than most."

"I know," he huffed in frustration. "Amy and Mum have drummed it into me. I can't help feeling overly protective. And my gorilla is constantly pushing and I'm not used to it. He is usually just there. I think if I could shift it would be easier," he muttered.

Sean looked at him in sympathy. "I'm sorry Kyle, we didn't know you were struggling. You should have said something. Rory and I can help with your Gorilla. You need a physical outlet like sparring or running because you can't fully shift."

"We'll get something sorted out for you starting tomorrow, okay?" said Rory, for once being serious.

"That would be great, because I think you might otherwise be wiping up blood and burying me the way I'm irritating Lottie," laughed Kyle, looking happier now that the boys were going to help him.

"Too right," I said just as I heard the front door open and Joel come down the hallway towards us.

"This kitchen smells fantastic, Sugar. I could smell the food all the way down the road and I'm starving," Joel said as he came through the back door and straight to me. He laid a long, hard kiss on my mouth. It went on long enough for my brothers to grumble at him, making us both laugh.

"Now you know how I feel when you two are mauling Amy," he said laughing at them as he went to the kitchen sink to wash his hands.

I started handing out the dishes filled with food. Just then the timer went off. I pulled the apple crumbles out and set them on the counter to cool down. There were six crumbles in all. I had also made a large chocolate cake and some jam tarts to accompany them.

"Do we have to wait for lunch?" muttered Sean, sniffing the air as I put the last crumble on the counter. "Those smell amazing, Julie."

I felt myself flush in pleasure. I loved cooking. Feeding my family and friends filled me with contentment.

I laughed at them as I sat at the table with them. I noticed that they hadn't dished up yet.

"Start dishing up, you guys. And, yes, you have to wait for the apple crumbles but I have some jam tarts you can have after breakfast."

"Just as well you're a shifter, Joel. If you were human you would be as big as a house with the way Julie feeds you," teased Kyle.

"I'm not complaining, your sister makes me very happy," smiled Joel while dishing up eggs onto my plate and then his.

As was usual with my family, there was lots of laughing and teasing while we ate. My tiger was purring in satisfaction as I listened to them chatting around our table.

JOEL

CHAPTER 12

I sat watching and listening to Julie and her brothers laugh and tease each other through breakfast and I felt at peace knowing she was happy.

Growing up in a house full of siblings and parents was hectic and, at times, I longed for peace and quiet. Then when I finally had it, I found that I hated it.

As I watched Julie slap Kyle's hand when he playfully went to steal her bacon, I had a vision of this table being filled with our offspring. Two boys and three girls. The girls were spitting images of my Sugar.

"Joel, Joel."

I shook myself and found them all looking at me in concern.

"Sorry, I zoned out for a minute, did you ask me something?"

"Rory wanted to know if you needed a hand with anything as you're taking today off?" explained

Julie, her brow furrowed in concern as she looked at me.

I shook my head. "No, I have it all sorted with the foreman. Deliveries are packed and have been sent and the ones for tomorrow are already on pallets waiting to go. I have given all the staff the rest of the day off. Today is for family and catching up."

My mate beamed a smile at me, her blue eyes sparkling with happiness. I knew she was looking forward to having everyone at our house. Jumping up, she started to clear the table only to be stopped by Kyle as he grabbed the plates from her.

"Sit your arse down, Julie. You know the rules. You cooked, we clean," he grumbled at her, pushing her back down in her chair.

"But... I don't mind," she muttered, scowling at him, making me smile at the look on her face.

"You may not mind but I do. I'm already in trouble at home, there's no way I won't be getting it in the ear if Mum and Lottie find that you cleaned up after cooking," he said, turning to the sink.

"And you two can help," he pointed at Sean and Rory who didn't seem to be inclined to move from the table.

"Why? We aren't the ones in trouble with our mate or our mother," smirked Sean.

"You will be if I tell Mum you shirked helping after I fed you," said Julie, poking him in his side, making him jump away.

"I think I preferred you meek and mild, squirt," said Rory, ruffling her hair as he got up.

"Would you stop," she said, slapping at him with one hand while pushing her hair out of her face with the other.

I was laughing at them and their carry on.

"Come on, you." I was grinning widely as I pulled her up from the table and into my arms. "Let's leave the help to wash up. You can come and spend some time with me before the hoards arrive."

"Hey, what do you mean by the help," muttered Sean, throwing a wadded dish towel at me, making me laugh as I ducked away from it. Grabbing Julie, I tossed her over my shoulder and ran out of the kitchen with her laughing all the way. I could still hear her brothers jeering from the kitchen when we got to the veranda.

I let Julie down off my shoulder as soon as we hit the veranda and held on to her hips to steady her as she laughed up at me.

As I took in her face that was alight with happiness, I felt a wave of love come over me. Dropping my mouth to her smiling lips, I nipped at them until she opened up inviting me in. I buried one hand in her hair, tilting her head back and pulling her tight against me with the other. I heard her tiger rumble. Gentling my kiss, I got an answering purr. I had got used to taking my cue from her animal on what would be tolerated when it came to how rough I could be with Julie during lovemaking. I had found in our mating that the two of them were constantly in sync, more so than any shifter I had known. I had an idea this was due to her upbringing.

Hearing a vehicle in the distance, I pressed a last kiss to the corner of her mouth before burying my face into her neck and breathing in her scent. Her fingers were combing through my hair and her tiger was purring loudly. My animal was answering with a rumbling growl that I felt deep in my chest.

I let out a sigh and muttered, "The masses are arriving."

She laughed softly and pressed a kiss to my cheek.

"Don't worry, they will all be gone by late this afternoon and then you will have me all to yourself."

I let go of her so we could turn and welcome the first lot of guests into our home. I watched as Anton and Luca pulled their bikes under the shade of the big tree. They were hyena shifter brothers and farmed about an hour away from us. They also handled all the online security checks we needed done when new staff were hired.

Tucking Julie into my side, I felt her arm go around my waist and give me a little squeeze. I didn't know how I got so lucky, but I was thankful everyday when I woke up with my mate, that Jett, Kyle and Lottie had brought her back with them.

JULIE

CHAPTER 13

Held securely in Joel's arms, I watched as two handsome men pulled up on motorbikes and parked under the trees. They both had dark hair and were muscular in build. They got off their bikes in a seamlessly choreographed move. Almost moving as one, it was obvious they were close as they walked up to the veranda. Pulling their sunglasses off and tucking them in their shirts. They looked up at us and both smiled showing deep dimples in their cheeks. If I hadn't known better, I would have said they were twins but I knew that Anton was the oldest of the two at thirty-four and Luca was thirty-one.

They bounded up the steps and grabbed us both in an exuberant hug. I couldn't help but laugh at them as they squished me in the middle.

"So good to meet you, Julie. And it's great to see this one looking much happier and relaxed than he has been the last couple of months," said Anton as he released us and dropped a kiss on my head, causing Joel to growl at him. He just laughed and shrugged, before ducking away from the slap that was aimed at his head.

"Excuse the idiot, Julie," grinned Luca. "You would have thought that he would have learned his lesson from Dex."

I couldn't help but like the two of them. They were happy for their friend and it showed.

I tapped Joel's stomach with the back of my hand, "Control yourself. I'm hugging them."

Joel pretended to grumble at me, "Fine, but make it quick."

Laughing at him, I hugged the two brothers. "Welcome to our home. I'm so glad to finally get to meet you. I've heard so much about all of you and you are the last ones for me to meet."

As I finished greeting them, I saw Annie's Land Rover pull up and Amy, Lottie and she got out.

Squealing, I left the males on the veranda and ran down to greet them.

"You're here," I said, hugging Annie tight. I hadn't seen her this week as she had been in town sorting out some staffing issues with her shop.

Letting her go, I hugged Amy, then turned to Lottie who was blossoming beautifully with her pregnancy. Now that we knew that she carried girls, everyone except Kyle had relaxed.

"Oh wow. Look at you, Lottie," I said, taking in her glowing cheeks, her green eyes shining with happiness. I pulled her into my arms for a hug. Feeling my nieces kicking, I put my hand on her belly, smiling as they pushed against it.

"Wow, they're pretty active, huh?" I asked.

"Tell me about it," grinned Lottie. "The only time they still is when Kyle is talking to them."

I grinned at her. "I hear he's in trouble with you all."

Lottie and Annie laughed as Amy said, "The man needs to take a chill pill, he's losing the plot."

I snorted with laughter at her comment.

I threaded my arm through Amy and Lottie's, Annie had gone on ahead of us.

"Come on, let's go up. Luca and Anton have just arrived. I've got to say, Amy and Lottie, not sure what is up with the women here that those two haven't been snapped up. They're gorgeous."

"Hey," grumbled Joel from the top of the stairs on the veranda, a grinning Luca and Anton on either side of him.

"Thanks, Julie. You're pretty hot yourself. Pity Joel saw you before us," laughed Luca as he ducked away from the punch Joel aimed at him.

It was all done in jest, you could see the closeness between them.

My brothers had come outside while they were all carrying on asking what we were laughing at.

"Just that the Russo's need to keep their hands to themselves," grumbled Joel.

I watched as Rory and Sean pulled Amy in for a hug and kiss. Things seemed to be calm between all of them for now.

While we were laughing and talking, the McGregors's and Moore's pulled up and were getting out of their Land Cruiser and walking up to the house.

Renee, Dex and Reggie were in the front, followed by Dex's brothers Falcon, Jett, Duke and Zane along with the Moore sisters Ava and Marie.

Reggie was in her last few weeks of pregnancy and was held protectively under her mate's arm as they came up the stairs to where we were all waiting.

It was mayhem for a while as greetings were exchanged. But once everyone was all sorted with drinks, Dex called the meeting to order. I had been to one other meeting and it always amazed me when they started listing all the different businesses that they ran and what was happening with them. Amy and Zane were in charge of keeping track of the accounts with Ava helping where she could.

After everyone had been updated in regard to the businesses, they moved on to the farms and what was needed. Falcon said he would be away for a while as he needed to fly to the city for a couple of lectures on some new veterinary procedures. Ava and Marie would be going with him so they could finish the last of their exams for the marketing and business courses they had been taking online. It was arranged for Sean and Rory to fly them in and go back in two weeks to collect them. This brought up the expected arrival of Reggie's sister who would become our full-time pilot.

I was listening with half an ear as none of it really concerned me. Jett and I had already updated everyone on the maternity clinics as well as the vaccination clinics we wanted to hold, but would be unable to until we had a pilot to fly us to the remote areas.

I tuned back in when Jett said that Anton and Luca had managed to find out what was happening with my family and why they were after me.

Jett turned and looked at me. "I'm sorry, hunny, it's not good news."

I nodded and sighed. "I figured it wouldn't be."

Snuggling further into Joel, I felt Annie hold my hand tightly in hers. I took a deep breath and said, "Okay, hit me with it."

Jett nodded at Anton who pulled some papers out of the briefcase he had brought with him and handed them over to me. It was a police report.

It was a report on a couple named James and Annette Baagh. They, along with a close friend had been found murdered after attending a show in the city. No arrests had been made and the case had been closed.

I was confused. Looking at Jett, I asked, "Who are they?"

"They were your real parents, Jule's. You were two years old and they had left you in the care of James's younger sister Rebecca so they could have an evening out in the city. It was supposedly a mugging gone wrong, but Anton and I think it was carefully planned by your aunt Rebecca and it was done for money. You come from a very rich family and your father further invested the family money leaving you a very wealthy heiress. I don't think he thought that the betrayal would come from his own family, but greed does funny things to people.

"With your parents dead, your aunt got guardianship of you as per the terms of the will. Which, by the way, was easy to get from the lawyer with your written permission. The lawyer is relieved you are okay. Apparently, he is not a fan of your aunt and has been trying to make contact with you but she keeps putting him off.

"Anyway, I digress. Your aunt got guardianship of you at the age of two. She was married and pregnant with her own cub. Her marriage was an arranged marriage into a family with political ties. Her husband is a complete waste of space and enjoys living the high life on your dime. Your aunt is in full control of all your assets and money including running the family company. The only thing she doesn't have control of is the large trust fund your parents left for you.

"The reason they are trying to get rid of you is because you are to inherit everything on your 26th birthday. Your aunt will be forced to retire from the head of the company on your 27th birthday, but will still receive a generous stipend to live on plus the house that she is living in at the moment.

"There is a clause in the will that should you mate or marry before your 26th birthday, then your mate or husband will share your inheritance equally except for the trust fund which would still solely be for you, Julie, unless there is a child.

Then the trust fund would be split equally between your offspring and yourself.

"This is why they are in a hurry for you to mate a male of their choosing so that they can keep control of your inheritance."

There was a stunned silence once Jett had finished as we absorbed all the information. I was both shocked and relieved that those that I had thought were my parents, weren't. No wonder I was so different from all of them. I could honestly say that except for Hannah, I didn't want to see any of them and I certainly didn't want their money. It had caused me nothing but misery. I told Jett as much.

He sighed as he looked at me. "Your dad must have thought about all of this because there is a stipulation that you can't give the company away. You can appoint a board to run it but you have to make quarterly appearances."

I wasn't happy at all. I looked at Joel and I knew he would support me in whatever I wanted to do.

Turning to Annie, all I saw in her eyes was love and support. Allowing my eyes to roam slowly around all the people gathered on my veranda, I saw that it didn't matter to them that we were all mixed shifters and, even though it shouldn't make sense, we were all friends and family. This group of shifters is who I trusted the most in my life.

"Let me get this straight," I said looking at Jett and Anton.

"I can appoint a board of my choice to run the company, one that I still don't know what it is by the way. Joel and I will share the inheritance, so that means we are both heads of the company and any of our children will benefit from the trust fund, which from my understanding is massive. Have I understood all that correctly?"

Anton nods and replies, "That about covers it."

Standing up, I slowly walked from one end of the veranda to the other while I thought.

Making a decision, I turn and look at them all, my eyes lingering on Joel.

"Are you able to get hold of the lawyer now and would he be open to talking to me over the phone or via video link?" I asked Jett.

Jett looked at Anton who nodded. Turning to Joel, Anton asked, "Can you bring me a laptop plus your satellite phone and I will get it sorted?"

As Joel got up to get the laptop, he stopped by me and pulled me into his arms for a hug. I instantly relaxed as the tension left my body.

"Whatever you need, Sugar, I will be here to support you," he murmured quietly into my ear.

I squeezed him tightly, then released him to go and get the laptop. Walking back to the group waiting for me, I dropped onto the sofa next to Annie. She wrapped an arm around me and my head found a place on her shoulder.

"It will be okay, baby," she says softly to me. "Your family is all here in this room and will support you all the way."

My throat clogs with tears as it hits me that I have lost so much from my aunt and her husband's greed. The last few months have been the happiest I have been in my life. That's all because I met Annie, her boys, and Joel.

I watched as Joel took the laptop and satellite phone over to Anton, who immediately sets it up.

After Jett placed the call a man in his late sixties answered the phone. Jett explained the situation and called me over to speak to the lawyer.

He smiled at me kindly through the screen. Behind him was a bookcase filled with books, and to the left a wall filled with certificates and pictures.

"Julie, it's so wonderful to finally meet you. My name is Phillip Yeats. Can I just say you look just like your mother? Jett and Anton have updated me and your parents would have been devastated with the way you have been treated," he remarks.

"Did you know my real parents then?" I queried.

He smiled sadly at me. "Yes, your father was my younger brother's best friend. Unfortunately, he died the same night they were all attacked. At least they all died together. That has been a great comfort to me."

"Are you saying that they were together as in a relationship between the three of them?" I asked.

"Yes, they were in a relationship. I have pictures that I can send to you if you want, but this one is my favourite," he said, holding up a picture of three people to the screen. I knew straight away that it's my mother and her mates. I look exactly like her, from my white hair with black streaks, to my purple-blue eyes, down to the shape of my body. The cleanly shaven, tall, well-muscled man on the right looked just like the woman I thought was my mother, but is in reality my aunt. The blond haired, bearded man on my mother's left was shorter but just as well-muscled. I could see the resemblance in the blond man to the man on the screen in front of me.

"Wow, I never knew," I say, not really sure how to feel. "Can I ask are you my aunt's lawyer as well as mine?"

"No," he says with a look of disgust on his face at the mention of my aunt.

"I am yours only, I have been trying to get in contact with you for two years but somehow your aunt always managed to block me. I was relieved when you packed up and disappeared with Jett. I reached out to them as soon as I could but, understandably, they wanted to check into my story first before allowing me access to you. I can't tell you how pleased I am with the support you have in your new friends and family. I'm glad you know what is going on, especially since you are already 26. Are you mated?"

"Yes, I am," I answered, beckoning Joel over and introducing him. "So, from what I can understand, I need to appoint a board of my choosing and this will revoke my aunt's rights to the company, which I understand from Jett and Anton's report is a chain of jewellery stores throughout several countries and continents. Is this correct?"

"Yes, that is correct and can I say it may be a good idea to make a will, if anything happens to you then your aunt keeps everything. If you want, I can do that today but you will need to come in and sign it as soon as possible."

I nod in acknowledgement and say we can do that but, first I wanted to set up my board. I mentioned all the names of my family and friends sitting behind me. The look on their faces showed their shock.

"Julie, are you sure," asks Dex.

Turning away from the computer I look at all of them.

"I'm sure. I trust all of you wholeheartedly. Dex, I have no clue how to run a company but all of you do. You all run your holdings and add to them constantly so I know that as a team, you can do this. As we each mate, we can add mates. This can be done on a one to one basis on whether they want to join or not. But this way I know that if anything happens to Joel or me then my parents legacy will continue to thrive. Would you all please serve on my board?" I ask.

A chorus of yes's are shouted out and Phillip laughs. He took down all the information he needed to set up the board. When I go in to sign my will, I'll pick up the documents and take them with me so that all my friends can read over them and sign where needed.

"Now that's done, can you update Joel's and my will? Have it state that should anything happen to us, everything will go to the members of the board unless we have children, then of course they will be our beneficiaries.

"I would like Annie to become guardian of any minor children we have along with my three adopted brothers.

"Can you also add a clause that should Joel or I, along with any of the board, die of anything not considered natural causes, then my aunt's stipend is to be cut off, her house is to be taken away from her and the company will be dissolved and sold off. Hopefully, that will stop her from trying to harm anyone else.

"Plus, my trust needs to be updated to show that I am with cub and in six months will give birth to two cubs or pups depending on who they take after."

You could have heard a pin drop before there was a great big roar and I was lifted off my chair by Joel as he pulled me into a tight hug. His eyes moist with tears, he kissed me hard, whispering in my ear *'how much he loved me'.* Then mum pulled me from his arms and into hers while he was surrounded by the others congratulating him.

JOEL

CHAPTER 14

I watched with pride as Julie listened and responded to what Jett and Anton had found out about her family. I was amazed at how she had taken everything in, then turned around and made decisions needed to stop these animals from taking what was rightly hers.

When she asked that our friends be on her board of directors, I could see they were shocked. But while she didn't know how the businesses were run, I knew she was a natural businesswoman just from the suggestions she made when she had helped me in the factory. Already my workload had been cut in half by some minor changes to the systems we used and some changes in how the packing was done.

Once we had all given the lawyer the information needed, we had moved on to her will. I wasn't worried about what it entailed since I wasn't interested in her money. My family's farm, as well as all our vested interests in the shared holdings we were partnered in, kept us very comfortable.

I wasn't really listening to the terms she was laying out until there was silence and you could have heard a pin drop. My mind finally realised what she had said, and I whooped as I jumped up, hugging her tight to me whispering how much I loved her.

My heart was full. I finally had to let her go as Annie was insistent about getting her hands on her daughter. My animal was doing circles in my head, making me laugh, even if it was making me slightly dizzy. Realistically, I knew that having young would happen quickly given how we couldn't keep our hands off each other, but for some reason I was still taken by surprise.

Amy threw herself at me in a tight hug, as twins we'd always had a strong bond. I could see that she was happy for us, but I also noted the tension around her eyes as she took in the happiness on her mates' faces as they congratulated their sister. Pulling my twin tighter into my embrace, my heart ached for my sister and her fears as a result of our upbringing.

"You need to speak to Rory and Sean, Amy," I whispered.

I felt her nod her head where it lay on my chest, looking down I saw her eyes were filled with tears.

"I know and I plan on doing it soon, I just hope they still want me after I speak to them," she whispered back.

A snort of laughter left me.

"Ames, those two are never letting you go no matter what. You need to be straight with them though. With Reggie, Lottie, and now Julie pregnant, you aren't going to be able to get away with what you have been doing for much longer. Besides, they know how much you love the kids that spend time with you on the farms. They're probably imagining all kinds of things and making it worse than it is. Have you thought about maybe speaking to someone about your fears?" I asked.

"Who would I speak to, Joel?" Amy asked.

"Mum, Joy, any of the aunts. I'm sure that you aren't the only one that has had these fears, sweetie," I suggested.

Giving me one last, long squeeze, she nodded again before letting me go. "Have I told you lately what a great big brother you are to me, Joel? Even if it's only by two minutes," Amy teased, smiling.

I laughed, tugging on her hair that was up in a ponytail. "Not recently, but I'm always up for you telling me how awesome I am."

This made her laugh out loud and I was pleased to see that some of the sadness disappeared from her eyes.

As I looked around my veranda at all of the people I not only considered friends but family, I marvelled at all the changes that seemed to have started as soon as Reggie mated with Dex. Our family had grown quickly since then. It was hard to believe that it had only been just a little over five months since Reggie's arrival.

I was looking forward to seeing what my parents thought about all the changes. I knew that some of the newer members of the family thought that they had been selfish to dump everything in my lap when it came to the farm. While it had been sooner than expected, I also knew my younger sister needed them more than I did. She needed their help getting settled into college in a different country. My parents were going to be thrilled to hear about all the new babies and I knew that they would consider them all their grandchildren, blood or not.

I couldn't wait for them to arrive in three weeks.

JULIE

CHAPTER 15

As we waved goodbye to the last of our family, I let out a contented sigh.

It had been a long emotional day, learning all the details about my birth family had hit hard. To find out that the couple I had always thought were my parents were not my biological parents was a huge relief. I was sad that I would not get to know my biological parents, but the family that had chosen me had shown me so much love in the last few months that the ache that I carried around in my heart had eased. Joel had completed that for me. Now with my own young growing in my womb, I felt nothing but pure happiness.

It had been a bit of a shock when my tiger, always so in tune with me, had thrown pictures of cubs at me. I knew they would both be boys but I wanted to share that with Joel before I said anything to anyone else.

Joel tightened the arms he had wrapped around me as we watched the last of the taillights disappear down our road.

He pressed a kiss to the side of my head.

"How are you doing, Sugar? There was a lot thrown at you today."

I sighed. Turning, I tucked my forehead against his throat, taking a minute before answering.

"I'm okay. I'm relieved that the awful woman is not my biological mother. I'm sad that my parents were murdered, but I'm so very thankful that my life brought me here to you, Annie and the boys. My life is so full now. I just wish we knew where Hannah was. I know Jett and Anton won't stop looking. I have a really bad feeling about her."

"Whatever happens, we will deal with it together. You aren't alone anymore. Day after tomorrow, we will go into town, sign the wills and documents and get them sent off. I'm glad that you don't have to go into the city to sign them. Our town is smaller, plus there are more people who know us and will let us know if there are any strangers around. I guess that's a bonus to living in a small town," said Joel.

I hummed in agreement, my eyelids getting heavy. I sighed and let go of him.

"Come on, let's shower and go to bed. It's going to be a busy couple of days and I, for one, need some time just with you before we have to deal with the mess my biological family has made of everything."

Locking up and switching the lights off, we went to our bedroom. Joel entered the bathroom and started the shower.

Stripping off, I groaned as I joined him. The hot water hit my shoulders, easing the tension that had built up during the course of the day.

My head dropped forward against the wall as Joel's soap-slicked hands massaged my tense shoulders. We didn't say anything as his hands softened and glided around to my breasts, massaging my sensitive nipples, then they glided over the lower part of my belly until they reached my pussy.

His fingers parted me as he circled my clit. I pushed my hips back against him and felt his hard cock pressing up against my back.

He tilted my head back on his shoulder before nipping the tendons of my neck with his teeth. His tongue laved over my mating mark on my shoulder, making me shiver in need.

I moaned as he thrust two fingers deep into my pussy, his other hand still busy circling my clit. I wasn't going to last much longer

"Joel," I moaned as my hips thrust faster against his fingers.

"I need you inside me when I come," I whimpered.

"Give me one first, Sugar," Joel demanded, his fingers working my clit faster. I could feel my cream dripping down my thighs and knew he could smell my arousal just like I could smell his.

"Bite me," I whispered, giving him my neck. His fangs bit down on my mating mark and I screamed as I came. I could feel my pussy clamp down hard on his fingers as wave after wave of my climax made its way through me. I slumped back heavily against him, my legs shaking from the power of my orgasm.

Joel switched off the shower before quickly picking me up and going through to our room. Putting me down on the bed, he pulled back and stood at the end. His eyes heated as he took me in lying naked and sprawled on our bed. He was gripping his hard cock in his hand, squeezing it so firmly that I could see his muscles bunching in his forearm and the tendons in his neck standing out in sharp relief.

Spreading my legs wider so he could see my cream wet and glistening on my inner thighs.

I asked him, "What are you waiting for?"

His eyes lifted to mine as he licked his lips. "I'm trying to decide if I should lick that pussy, fuck it or both."

I moaned as heat spread throughout me. I brought my legs together and rubbed my thighs trying to stop the ache.

"Both it is," Joel rasped as he bent and licked me from back to front. Flattening his tongue, he lapped at my clit making me squirm and pant with need. I could feel another orgasm coming on, my thighs tightening around his head, my hands gripping and pulling at his hair. I came with a high keening sound as he thrust a finger into me and bit down hard on my clit.

Just as I was coming down from that orgasm, I felt him thrust his hard cock into me, making my eyes roll back in my head.

He stilled his movements and I opened my eyes to find him watching me.

"You good, Sugar?"

I nodded and gave him a smile as he slowly moved out of me before pushing back in slowly, making me shiver as his cock rubbed along the sensitive walls of my pussy. I could feel him growing in my core and I knew soon we would be locked together as he came. It didn't happen every time, but when it did, I loved it because it meant he had to stay with me a while.

Pulling him down onto me so that I could reach his mouth I kissed him softly. My hands ran through his hair and down his back. Lifting my legs, I wrapped them around his hips and pulled him in tight.

His arms tightened around my back, easing me upright so that our chests rubbed erotically against one another as he sat back on his heels. His hips continued their slow thrusts and he groaned into my neck as he came.

I sighed in bliss, my body humming with pleasure as I pressed a kiss to the side of his head.

I had never felt so peaceful.

JOEL

CHAPTER 16

It had been a busy week, we had gone into town to meet up with Julie's lawyer Phillip and had set up everything including the new wills and her new board of directors.

He had brought a few personal mementoes with him for Julie, such as pictures of her parents and some of her mum's jewellery that had been in his brother's safe that he had kept for her, hoping to one day make contact. She was overwhelmed to have these with her and, after the business side was done, I had suggested that maybe the two of them would like to go for lunch to catch up while I went and did some farm business. I knew Julie would be safe as Luca and Anton were sitting at the bar keeping an eye out. We were all going to spend the night at a local hotel in town before going back to the farm. Anton and Luca were going to leave after us to make sure no-one followed us home.

We weren't expecting anything to happen just yet, but I had a feeling when the will and its changes were made known to her aunt that in the next week, the shit was going to hit the fan. I, for one, couldn't wait so that we could get on with our lives.

Finishing my business, I went back to the restaurant to meet with Julie.

I was looking forward to taking her out this evening. After dinner, we were meeting with Anton and Luca at a local club owned by Ava and Marie that they had bought about a year ago.

I walked towards where she was saying goodbye to Phillip who was leaving as I entered. I stopped him on his way out to say my own goodbye before making my way to the bar where Anton and Luca were chatting with Julie. As I approached, she threw her head back and laughed at something Luca said. Watching how radiantly happy she was took my breath away. I slipped my arms around her and pulled her tight into me, pressing a kiss to her temple, breathing in her unique scent.

"Joel," she murmured, leaning back into me.

"Sugar, are you ready to go up to our room?" I asked.

"Yep, I could do with a nap," she said, yawning. "Growing your babies is pretty exhausting," she muttered.

I chuckled, giving her a last squeeze before taking her hand to lead her away.

Nodding at Luca and Anton, I asked, "Are you two still going with us to the club tonight?"

"Yeah, we will see you there at about nine. I've reserved a booth in the VIP section so Julie won't get jostled too much," replied Anton.

"Thanks, man," I said, giving his shoulder a squeeze.

"See you both later," Julie said as we moved off towards the lifts.

"Jules," Anton acknowledged with a chin lift.

"Later, babe," added Luca with a smirk at me.

Narrowing my eyes at him, I give him the finger behind Julie's back, making them both laugh.

"How was your meeting sweetheart?" I asked Julie as we reached the elevator, only the two of us were waiting to get on.

Taking a proper look at her, I made note of the dark circles under her eyes. I knew she hadn't been sleeping well the last couple of days and I wished that this was all over and done with. But until her aunt receives the paperwork and we find her missing cousin, things will be stressful.

She sighed before tightening her arms around me and resting her head on my chest.

"Honestly, I just want it over. I'm worried about Hannah. It's weird knowing she is my cousin and not my sister. I'm so happy to have the pictures and jewellery from my parents but sad too. Sad for our children, they won't know my family. Sad for me and all that I missed, and sad for them that their family murdered them for their money. I'm concerned about having the company come to me and being responsible for all those people and their jobs. What happens if I can't run a company that size and keep them all employed?" she asks.

"That's a lot you have going on in your head, Sugar, how about we break it down some?

"First, we will find Hannah and she will always be your sister. Second, it's okay to be sad and we will find out as much as we can about your parents and tell our children about them. Plus, you have a family in Annie and the boys and trust me my family will more than makeup for any family you are missing, especially my mum," I said, making her giggle. My mum is a force of nature.

"Third, the company has managers in charge and I can't imagine that your aunt goes to each one on a regular basis. Once all the paperwork is transferred, we can have an audit done and have a look at the financials. You have a whole family that is on your board of directors and they all have their own talents. We can visit all the different branches so that you can meet everyone and see what needs to be done. Start with the ones that are not performing and work your way up," I advised as the elevator dinged for our floor.

"But first, all you have to do this afternoon is take a nap. Then later on, I have booked a beauty therapist to come to our room and pamper you."

"God, you are an amazing mate, I don't know how I got so lucky," she murmured, kissing my cheek.

Unlocking the door, I entered first to check the room before allowing her inside where she immediately flopped down tiredly on the bed.

Closing the curtains, I adjusted the air conditioning before checking on her. I smiled, noticing she is already sound asleep. Pulling the covers back, I removed her shoes and tucked her in before dropping a kiss on her forehead.

Closing the door, I settled in the lounge to research how many branches are in the businesses and check on the basic financials so that we have a better idea of how much travelling we would have to do in the next couple of months.

JULIE

CHAPTER 17

We were back on the farm and I couldn't be happier. While I had enjoyed getting pampered, dressed up, and having dinner at a great local restaurant, it was also exhausting because I hadn't realised how many people knew Joel, Anton, and Luca. It seemed wherever we went, they were stopped by people wanting to catch up with them.

It was worse when we got to the nightclub, our booth seemed to get fuller by the hour. The dirty looks I had gotten from some of the women amused me. It seemed they weren't happy that Joel was off the market. Joel had kept me close. So close that I didn't get to leave his lap after one of the human men held my hand too long when I was introduced.

We'd been bracketed by Anton and Luca on either side of us. They both had women hanging off them and I knew they wouldn't be going home by themselves tonight.

Ava and Maire had both come to check on us and had stayed for a while until they were called away.

They were busy training a new manager to run the club for the times when they would be called away to the farm for business.

I had been impressed with all that they had achieved. They were both in their early twenties but, like the others, seemed to have a firm grasp on running their business. Such a lifestyle was not for me, but they seemed happy. I was far happier on the farm nursing people who needed me.

Jett and I had a busy week planned. We were doing vaccinations at a village about two hours from us. Since we were leaving at 4 a.m. tomorrow morning, I was busy getting inventory and stock done so that we could load up the vehicle when Jett arrived. He would be spending the night with us and I was looking forward to catching up with him.

Joel was coming with us. He didn't want to let me travel far without him now that I was pregnant. I was happy to have him along. Amy and her mates were coming tomorrow to run the farm for him.

Seeing Jett's Land Cruiser coming through the main gate, I waited for him at the door of the clinic while he parked.

He jumped out with a huge smile on his face. He grabbed me and hugged me tightly before swaying us from side to side.

"How's my favourite nurse?" he boomed in my ear. I laughed at him, he was always cheerful and you couldn't help but feel happy in his presence.

"I'm your only nurse," I said laughing.

A rumbling growl came from behind Jett. Joel had walked up when he had seen Jett pull in. Joel pulled me out of Jett's arms and tucked me tight into his side.

"What is it about my friends that always seem to want to hug you?" Joel grumbled, before turning to Jett and offering his hand.

"That's because she is awesome," Jett stated. I felt my face flush at the praise.

"Come on, let's get everything loaded up," I said, moving to the clinic door to show them where everything was packed for tomorrow.

"We'll load up," Joel commented as he grabbed a chair from my desk and took it outside to put on the small veranda. "You sit here and supervise."

I sat and got comfortable. It wasn't a hardship to watch the two of them load up the vehicle. The view got even better when they took off their shirts, their chests glistening with sweat in the fading summer light

JETT

CHAPTER 18

It had been a long day, we had been on the road since 4 a.m. to travel to one of the more remote villages. I knew we would still have to travel this way even with the planes since there was nowhere we could land a plane anywhere close by.

I was going to bring up at the next meeting that we should look into the cost of purchasing a helicopter for trips such as these to save on travel time.

I was happy with the progress we had made today in the vaccination clinic as well as treating minor ailments. Having Julie helping had made the day go quickly and we were nearly done. I still thought that she was the best thing to have happened to all of us. I had been hoping that she was a mate for one of my brothers, but seeing her and Joel together was just as good for me. He seemed so much lighter since the two of them had mated.

Joel was busy repacking the vehicle. It had been great having him with us today, he had helped where he could. I had insisted that everyone be qualified in basic first aid, as we all lived in remote areas and we all had a lot of staff on our payroll. That allowed him to deal with minor injuries, making this day go much quicker.

Usually when I did a clinic like this, I was here until nearly 10 p.m. before I even thought about packing up. But with the three of us working together, the day had flown by and the sun was just starting to set, lighting the sky up in a beautiful red. There were bats just starting to come out and you could see them swooping through the twilight. As I stood there sucking down a bottle of water while watching the sun fade, I thought to myself *'There was nothing quite like an African sunset.'*

Joel called out and I saw that Julie was tucked up in the back of the Land Cruiser, a pillow pushed up against the window, her head resting on it. She was already asleep by the looks of it.

Opening the passenger door, I jumped in, ready to leave the site.

"Let me know when you've had enough and I will take over driving," I said to Joel. Getting a chin lift in acknowledgement, I got comfortable and before I knew it, I was asleep.

We had been travelling for about an hour when I was woken up by Joel stopping the vehicle.

"What's up?" I asked.

"Your phone has been ringing non-stop since we hit the signal area. I think we need to check it," Joel replied, getting out to dig in the bags behind the seats until he found my phone.

Jumping back in the vehicle, he handed it to me.

"It's Anton," I muttered as I hit the button to phone him back.

"Hey A, what's going on?" I queried, putting the phone on speaker phone for Joel to hear the conversation.

"Shit's hit the fan, Jett. Julie's family got the notification from the lawyers this afternoon and there's a lot of movement at the house that we have under surveillance. The aunt went straight to the bank and found herself unable to access any of the accounts. From the reports coming in, she made a fool of herself by throwing a fit in the manager's office," said Anton.

"Any news on her sister's whereabouts?" questioned Joel.

"That's why I'm calling. They sent a picture of her sister to her messenger account. And it's not good, brother. She looks like she has been tortured and starved. They have her hanging up naked from the rafters and I can make out a cage behind her. They are demanding that Julie reinstates everything and then they will release her," Anton growled out.

I could hear the anger in his voice, we didn't take kindly to females being mistreated in our family.

I heard a disgusted snort from behind and Julie poked her head between the seats.

"I'm not giving them anything," she said angrily. "They will probably kill Hannah anyway. Do we have a way of tracking them?" she asked.

"Busy working on that now," replied Anton. "We have narrowed it down to a specific area and I can see from the picture that it looks like they are holding her in an old tobacco barn. I recognise the press in the background. We are looking at the farms owned by Hannah's family. We are focusing on one location right now since they seem to own a lot of acreage in that area."

"What area are you looking at?" Julie asks.

"The lower Mwana area," replies Anton.

"Do either of you have enough internet bars to pull me up a map of the area?" Julie asks.

Joel nods and pulls up the area on the phone and hands it to Julie.

I watch as she messes around with it a little before she makes a humming noise.

"I remember a conversation I overheard once about a tobacco farm belonging to my uncle's family that they were going to abandon as there wasn't enough water on it," Julie says.

I keep my gaze on her as she looks at the map on the phone, something catches her attention, and she zooms in.

"Here," She hands me the phone. "This is the farm."

"Are you sure?" I ask her as I send the coordinates to Anton.

She nods at me. "Yeah, that's the farm. Is there any way to have it checked out to confirm if that's where they are?"

"That's not too far from our place," Anton states when he receives the coordinates. "Luca and I will check it out. Give us a couple of hours, once we have confirmation be ready to move."

I looked at Joel, before making a call to Dex and filling him in. We decided that we would all meet at Joel and Julie's place and make a plan on how we would get Hannah out if that was where she was being held.

JULIE

CHAPTER 19

Once Jett finished the phone call with Anton, Joel didn't waste any time getting us back to the farm.

We hadn't been home for more than half an hour when the others started arriving. First came Mum, followed by Kyle, Lottie, Sean, Rory and Amy. Close behind them were all the MacGregors and Renee Moore.

Once we were all there, Dex pulled out a big map from a tube he had been carrying. The map was of the area I had looked at. I marked the location of the farm where I thought they were keeping Hannah.

"Okay, this is what is going to happen once we hear back from Anton and Luca," Dex said, looking at all of us gathered on the veranda.

"First, those of us who can shift will go in as our animals on foot. It will be quicker than driving since we can cut straight across the land rather than using the roads. Lottie, Kyle, and Renee, you bring the medic bus. By looking at the damage done to Hannah in this photo, Jett is going to need all the medical supplies we can bring.

"Jett, you and Julie need to go and make sure that the bus is fully equipped with whatever you might need. Thank fuck, we keep it here rather than at our place," he added.

I nodded at him and got up from where I had been sitting on Joel's lap. Jett followed me out and we made our way down to the vehicle known as the medic bus.

It used to be a minibus, but it had been modified to be used on the back roads and had everything you would usually find in an ambulance. It didn't get used very often. But it came in handy if we needed to take someone to town that didn't need to be flown out. We went through the inventory and made sure it was fully stocked with all we would need. I then went ahead and filled each of us with a small first aid kit that we could carry around our necks to tide us over until the others arrived with the bus.

Once Jett was satisfied we had all that we needed, we got in the vehicle and drove it up to the house. Joel and Annie were bringing out cool boxes and extra blankets. I was so worried and distracted that I hadn't even thought about food and drinks.

Joel was at my door as soon as we pulled up to the house. He helped me out and pulled me into his arms for a tight hug. I shoved my face into his neck and breathed in his scent. My shoulders relaxed as I took in his familiar aroma. My tiger had been restlessly pacing about in my head since we had heard about Hannah, but she eased back once Joel had us in his arms.

I returned his hug, before looking up at him. He framed my face with his hands and studied my face, his animal showing in his eyes both checking on us.

"How are you holding up, Sugar?" Joel questioned me gently.

I blinked fiercely to stop the tears welling up. There will be time for tears later once we have Hannah.

"I'm okay, Joel, or as okay as I can be now. I can't promise I won't fall apart once we have Han, but until then I am doing okay," I replied.

A phone rang on the veranda and Dex picked it up, hitting the speaker so we could all hear.

"Luca! Talk to me," barked Dex.

"She's here, and brother she is in bad shape. You need to get here soon. Anton is going up the wall. It started as soon as he saw her. I'm holding him back for now, but I'm not sure how much longer I can keep him contained. For now, she is locked in a cage and seems to be unconscious, but I can't promise that I will be able to hold him back if they start up beating her again. Make sure you bring the bus, we are going to need it," stated Luca. The fun-loving male I had gotten used to was gone and in his place was a furious male.

From the conversation, I understood that Anton must be Hannah's mate and I knew it would be hard for him to keep himself contained while his mate was being hurt.

"How many are we looking at going against, Luca?" asked Falcon.

"No more than seven at any one time. They are pretty lax with security which is how we managed to get so close. The only problem I foresee is that they are all armed with AK47s, but if we can take them by surprise, it shouldn't be a problem," Luca responded.

"Stop fucking talking and get your asses here ASAP. I'm not fucking waiting if they start in on her again," growled Anton darkly.

"On our way brother, just hang in there. Those of us that can shift will be coming across country. We will be there within an hour. Renee, Lottie and Kyle will come with the bus, but it is going to take them at least two and half to three hours before they will make it. Julie and Jett are bringing basic first aid and will be with us," Dex replied while starting to strip.

The rest of us on the veranda follow suit, our clothes in bundles in front of us. Before long every single one of us was standing in our animal form. Renee, Lottie and Kyle went around hanging our clothing bundles around our necks so that we could change into them when we got to the farm where they were holding Hannah.

Dex and his brothers took off in front of us since they knew the way through the bush. The rest of us followed along behind them. If this wasn't a rescue mission, I would have enjoyed us all being together, although I'm sure it would have looked strange if anyone saw us like this.

Leopard, Wild Dog, Tiger and Gorilla's all running together. Birds flew up as we charged along, monkeys screamed at us, and my brothers barked back at them in reply. This startled a group of Impala that had been lazily grazing in the sun into stampeding away.

We were in a hurry and weren't being quiet, but I knew the closer we got the slower we would go so as not to alert them of our approach.

About forty-five minutes into our run, the MacGregors slowed down to a walk, their sides heaving and sweat glistening on their fur.

While I had kept up with them, my family, Amy, and Joel had fallen behind. My brothers had taken to the trees where they could, this had them keeping up for a while as they moved faster in the treetops. My mother had opted to stick with Joel and Amy.

As we waited for everyone to catch up, I noticed that we were all looking tired. We had pushed hard to get here as quickly as we could and, while most of us could run for a long time, we weren't built to run as hard and as quickly as we had.

Making a decision, I changed quickly back to human.

"Change back and drink some water before we carry on," I said, pulling my water bottle out from my bundle of clothes around my neck.

Joel, Amy, and my mother arrived just as I finished talking. Joel changed smoothly from animal to human in the blink of an eye. Kissing my cheek, he grabbed his bottle and drank until it was finished before returning the empty to his bundle of clothing. While doing this, I had pretended not to notice that he had put his big body between me and the other males. My eyes flicked to Sean, Amy and Rory. I noticed that they had done the same thing.

Amy rolled her eyes at me, making me snigger softly. As shifters, we didn't have an issue with nudity, but it seemed our males didn't like us being naked in front of the others.

Once we had all finished drinking, we studied the map that Dex had out.

"We aren't far now, maybe twenty more minutes. We're going to have to go in slower, we don't want to alert them. This is where Luca said he and Anton are waiting for us," he said pointing to a spot on the map before folding it up and putting it back into his bundle.

"Falcon knows this part of the country best, so he's going to take the lead here on in. We can make a plan on how we are going to proceed once we reach Anton and Luca," Jett informed us.

Nodding, we changed back into our animals and carried on at a much slower pace than we had been.

It wasn't long before we met up with Anton and Luca.

Luca looked relieved to see us as we all slowly walked up to them. I could see that Luca was right. Anton was about to come out of his skin. He had stripped off his shirt and was only in a pair of shorts, his powerful chest was wet with sweat.

He was vibrating from rage, and I could see he was fighting a constant battle with his animal not to change. It was pushing him hard if the constant growling and part shift of his hands were any indication.

ANTON

CHAPTER 20

Listening impatiently to Luca as he spoke to Dex and the others about how they were going to make it here as quickly as possible, I finally interrupted them as they didn't seem to get the urgency of the situation.

My mate was in there wounded, broken, and starving from the treatment she had received from those she had called family.

My animal was pushing at me constantly to go in and get her. I was barely holding him back, and knew that if they started hurting her again, then there would be no holding him back, even if it meant getting ourselves hurt.

I still was in shock at finding her. When Luca and I had started out this evening after receiving intel from some of our guys that were keeping an eye on Julie's family, I figured it would be a quick trip out and back. I hadn't expected to be hit by the mating urge as soon as I saw her lying on that dirty blanket locked in a cage that was nearly too small for her. The only light in the dark room came from a small kerosene lamp in the corner of the barn.

There was a blanket covering half her lower body, leaving her uncovered. I could see the welts and dried blood. Her feet were in the same condition, caked in dirt and blood. It looked as if they had beaten her with something small and thin on the soles of her feet.

Our animals healed us quickly, but with the constant beatings and starvation her body couldn't keep up. She was so thin that I could see each of her ribs. Her back and feet would be a mass of scars once she was healed.

As if sensing she was being watched, she slowly sat up, pulling the threadbare blanket over her to conceal the rest of her nakedness. With her hand, she pushed back the thick swathe of red and gold hair from her face. A pair of green eyes, dulled with exhaustion and pain, looked straight at me. Her eyes widened with surprise. I put a finger to my lips in the universal sign for quiet. She nodded her head slightly in understanding.

I hated to leave her, but I needed to get to Luca, and let the others know that she was here.

After hours of waiting for the others to arrive, I felt immense relief when they slowly emerged from the trees. I waited impatiently as they changed and got dressed. I felt Luca's hand on my shoulder tighten in support.

All I wanted to do was run in and sweep her up in my arms and take her somewhere safe where I knew she would never be hurt.

Mentally chiding myself for not paying attention, I tuned back into the conversation that was going on around me.

"Luca has given us the shift changes that he has been able to see so far. They seem to change shifts every hour on the door that Hannah is locked behind. What we need is a distraction of some sort," Dex said looking around at us.

"What's in the shed to the far side of the property?" Rory asked.

"I'm not sure," replied Luca. "We didn't get to check out all of the property. Once we found her, we didn't want to risk being seen until you all were closer in case shit hit the fan."

Rory nodded in understanding. "Sean and I are going to check it out. If it's suitable, we could set it on fire as a distraction while some of you get into the barn to get Hannah out."

The two of them melted into the darkness without a sound. They weren't gone ten minutes before they were back.

"Their security is really shit," said Sean quietly. "They are all human from what I can tell and, so far, the most dangerous thing about them is the bad way they are handling their firearms. A couple of them are drunk and that's dangerous. Also, if we're going to move, we need to do it now. Listening in, it seems that the brother and father are on their way here to dispose of the problem. My bet is once they have killed Hannah, they will be leaving the country with whatever they can scrape together."

I growled in anger at the mention of them killing my mate.

Rory looked at me in sympathy.

"We'll get her out of there before that happens brother," he promised me.

"Best bet, we set a small fire against the shed. There is no chance of it spreading since there's nothing close by. Once they rush to that, we disarm the guards on the door and get Hannah out. Once she is safe, we set up a trap for the brother and father," Sean declared.

We are all in agreement with that and it was decided that Julie, Jett and myself would be the one's going in to get Hannah. What surprised me the most was the blood thirsty look in Annie's eye when her boys tried to get Amy and her to stay in trees and wait for us.

She snorted at them in disgust. "Let me remind you boys that before I took off with you two, I was being trained as the enforcer for our troop. And while I haven't had to fight anyone in a while, it doesn't mean I can't if I must."

With that, she turned to look at Dex and the others. "Where do you need Amy and me?" she questioned.

A chastened Rory and Sean headed off to start the fire and we all got into place and waited. We watched as the fire started and grew, burning the shed. Men started shouting and running towards the fire. The guard in front of the barn didn't move but did turn and watch. I snuck up behind him and grabbed his head, giving it a twist, I heard a crack, and he went limp against me. Laying him down on the ground, I carefully opened the door, peering inside. I looked at the shadows but couldn't sense anybody else inside.

"Amy," I whispered, looking at my friend in the darkness as she came forward. "Keep watch at the door and let us know if anyone approaches." She nodded and disappeared into the shadow by the door while Jett and Julie pushed past her. Julie made straight for the cage on the floor where Hannah was now lying down.

I pulled the dead guard in after me and shoved him into the corner of the barn.

"Han," Julie whispered quietly, her hand gently shaking her sister's shoulder. Hannah hissed slightly in pain at the movement but didn't wake up.

"We need to unlock this gate," Julie said.

Going to the cage, I looked at the lock. Grabbing it in my hand, I crushed it, wanting to get to my mate as quickly as possible.

"Found the key," Jett said, turning around and holding it up. Seeing the remains of the lock on the floor, he shrugged and threw them on the floor. "Guess we won't be needing them."

Unable to wait any longer, I crawled into the cage with my mate and gently pulled her into my arms. She whimpered in pain at the movement.

"Here wrap her in this and get rid of that blanket," Julie said, passing me the space blanket she had in her first aid kit.

I wrapped it gently around Hannah. Glancing at her front I saw that the damage they had done to her wasn't only on her back, they had whipped her there too.

Taking a deep breath to control my anger, I finished wrapping her up and passed her out the cage to Jett. He stood up with her in his arms. When I was standing outside the cage, he handed her to me with no questions asked.

Everything had gone quiet outside, so I assumed that our group had everything well in hand. I took her to where Julie had set up a table with the other space blanket and the limited first aid they had brought with them.

"Put her on here, Anton, and stand by her head while Jett and I assess her and see what is going on. I think they have drugged her which is why she is so unresponsive. A blessing for her," Julie mumbled as she started unwrapping the blanket, hissing when she noted the amount of damage on her sister's skin, her hip bones jutting out, showing how thin she was.

Jett was looking at her feet and shaking his head at the sight of them.

"I think the best thing we can do is make her comfortable and wait until we are home. We're going to have to irrigate and clean all these cuts. I think it will be easier to do that in a bathtub. I'm worried about her feet. It looks like they kept her in a state of starvation and as she healed, they tortured her again until her body couldn't keep up with the healing," Jett murmured quietly.

"I'm going to kill them all," Julie declared, bending to press a kiss on her sister's forehead.

My beast rumbled in my chest in agreement. She looked up at me, her violet eyes glowing in the dimness of the barn. "Oh, you can definitely help me, big guy," she muttered, patting my hand.

Wrapping her in blankets, we got Hannah as comfortable as we could. She was still unconscious but both Jett and Julie said this was better for her. They couldn't risk giving her anything else as they weren't sure what she had been drugged with but assumed it was an animal tranquiliser of some kind.

I watched from the door as the others piled the bodies of the guards behind the barn and took up their places acting as guards. I was standing guard in front of the now closed barn doors. We were hoping that Julie's brother and father wouldn't realise it wasn't their guards until it was too late.

I couldn't wait to get my hands on them and have them suffer the same fate as the beautiful woman inside.

I straightened as Joel gave a low whistle with his wild dog hearing he had picked up the sound of a vehicle way before any of us.

"Is it the bus?" asked Luca.

"No, this is a different engine. I think it may be Julie's brother and father," answered Joel quietly.

We all watched as the Mercedes they were driving came to a stop and the doors opened. Quietly I opened the doors to the barn and silently slipped inside as they walked towards me. They were arguing about what to do with Hannah. The brother was against killing her, saying it won't benefit them in any way and it may just increase the already difficult situation they were in even more.

They hadn't noticed the change in the guards.

I shook my head in disgust, they're poor excuses for shifters. Not once did they scent the air to confirm that all was as it should be and that no strangers were around. My guess was they were so confident that they were going to get away with what they had planned, they never thought that anyone would look for Hannah.

I had left the barn doors open when I had made my way inside and waited for them in the darkness. Julie was opposite me, her purple eyes gleaming and her tiger pushing to the front. I noticed her hands were part shifted and she had been steadily growling softly.

"You need to quieten your tiger, Julie, or they will hear her growling," I whispered.

Instantly, the growling cut off.

The two men continued arguing as they came towards the barn, my blood was boiling as I heard what the father had planned for his daughters.

As the first man, the father, entered the barn, I grabbed him and held my hand over his mouth to stop him shouting out and pulled him into the shadows of the barn. His son entered, not long after him and Julie and Annie grabbed him. He was no match for the two pissed off shifter females.

"Take them over to the chains," Julie said, dragging her brother over to them.

The rest of our family came in through the doors to watch. Dex and Luca tossed a chain over a beam above them, then helped us restrain them. Once retrained we hooked them up to the chain with the hooks that had been hanging on the wall of the barn. We pulled on the chain until their feet were barely touching the floor. We secured the end of the chain to the bolts on the side of the barn wall left there just for this purpose.

The whole time we had been securing them, they had been shouting and pleading until finally Jett had enough and shoved pieces of the dirty blanket in their mouths to shut them up.

Our family surrounded Julie and I as we looked at the pieces of scum hanging from the chains in front of us.

Out of the corner of my eye, I saw Julie pick up the discarded riding crop that they had been using to whip Hannah with. It was coloured in dark brown splotches that was more than likely Hannah's dried blood.

Julie turned to look at Annie and Amy who were standing in the corner leaning against the table that Hannah lay on.

"If you two want to leave, now is the time because I can't say once I start on them that I will be able to stop. All I ask is that you take Hannah with you if you do decide to leave and wait outside," Julie stated, her tiger showing in the elongated pupils of her eyes.

Annie waved her off and said, "You and Anton do what you have to, sweet girl. Amy and I will take care of your sister until either you are done or the others arrive with the bus, whichever is quickest."

Julie nodded and looked at Joel who was standing next to her. Joel dropped a kiss on her forehead and uttered, "Do what you need to and when your arms get tired let me know and I will finish it for you."

Turning she gazed at Dex and Luca who were still standing in front of the two men. "Strip them," she ordered, tightening her hand on the crop.

Between the two of us, we worked them over for six hours, only resting while they healed before starting back up again. All the while, they begged and pleaded but none of us could find any sympathy for them after we had seen the state they had left Hannah in.

About two hours in, the bus arrived and Jett, Annie and Amy moved Hannah to that to make her more comfortable. That left Joel, Dex, Falcon, Duke, Zane, Sean, and Rory in the barn with us.

Finally, I felt the rage leave my body, my arm hanging limply by my side. The two men hanging in front of me were not even recognizable anymore. They had fallen silent about four hours in and had stopped healing in the fifth hour. Julie was being held in Joel's arms, exhaustion and sadness clear in her eyes, her entire body, including her hair and face, covered in blood.

I knew I probably looked the same. I could feel it dripping from my hands and my face was sticky with the residue of it.

"You done?" Dex questioned from where he was leaning against the wall of the barn, his arms folded across his chest.

I nodded and looked at Julie, my brow raised in query. She nodded back.

"We're done," I replied.

"What do you want done with them?" queried Duke, looking at the bloody mess in front of us.

Julie pushed out of Joel's arms and, lightning fast, she partially shifted. She swiped her claws across her uncle's throat, slicing it open, blood dripping to the floor. We watched in silence as life left his eyes. Following suit, I dispensed with his son in the same way.

"Burn them, and the bodies outside the barn to the ground," replied Julie before turning and walking outside. I followed her, knowing my brothers would deal with it.

As the two of us left the building, I noticed that the sun was just rising in the sky. Julie and I sighed in unison as we took in the rising sun. Grinning, I said to Julie, "It's going to be a beautiful day."

She returned my grin with a small smile and replied, "Yes, it is."

JULIE

CHAPTER 21

Anton and I washed up and threw our blood-stained clothes into the barn before it was set on fire.

We stayed only long enough to ensure that the fire didn't spread and once it was a smouldering heap of ash, we got into the vehicles that the others had arrived in. It was Renee who had decided it was better to bring more than just the medic bus. And for that I was grateful, there was no way I felt like going back home on foot.

I snuggled into Joel on the back seat of the Land Rover that Renee was driving. I closed my eyes. I was sad that my family was so messed up that they thought it was okay to starve and torture my little sister who had done nothing other than protect me. It wasn't in me to hurt someone just for the sake of it. I knew what I had done to them was going to weigh on me some. But I couldn't help but feel lighter now that the threat to Hannah and me had been eliminated.

I tucked my face into the crook of Joel's neck, breathing in his scent.

The last thing I remembered is Joel pressing a kiss to my forehead as I slipped into sleep.

JOEL

CHAPTER 22

Julie had been fierce and had looked like a warrior woman covered in blood as Anton and she beat the hell out of the pieces of shit that had given the order for the torture of her younger sister.

And while I knew that they got everything they deserved, Julie at her heart was a nurturer and hurting someone or something was not in her nature. I wondered how much this would cost her mentally. I would be keeping a close eye on her in the next few weeks and make sure that she got whatever she needed to help her make peace with it.

Pressing a kiss to her forehead, I felt her body get heavier as she relaxed into sleep curled up on my lap.

JULIE

CHAPTER 23

I was in my favourite place sitting on the veranda steps watching the sun slowly descending in the sky. I admired the garden and how different it looked now to how it had looked when I first pulled into this driveway just over three months ago. The beautiful green lawn spread out amongst the trees and there were bright flowers in the flower beds.

So many changes over the short period of time had me thinking back over the last few weeks. They had been busy as hell. We got my sister home safely. Then the long road of recovery for her began. Anton basically moved into our house. He didn't want to be far away from Hannah.

I was worried about my sister. She was quiet and withdrawn. Annie assured us that with time, love, and patience she would get back to her old self. The scars on her body remained as a reminder of all that she had endured. Jett was looking around to see if there was someone we could trust for her to talk to, but so far he hadn't had any luck in our shifter community.

Joel's parents have arrived and were happily settled in their wing. They were over the moon at the fact that in a few short months they would be grandparents.

Having them stay with us was a weight off our shoulders. It left me with more time to help Jett with the clinics and Joel had more time on the farm with less administrative work to do since he happily dumped it all in his father's lap.

They weren't going to be with us full-time. They wanted to travel and visit their other children but decided to use the farm as their homebase.

After much discussion, it was decided that the little shop selling our ground coffee and whole beans at their holiday home on the coast in South Africa was doing so well, that they were looking at expanding and opening shops in different locations. That meant they would travel around more. Joy, one of Joel's siblings living in America, had said she would be interested in running the one they opened there once the location was decided.

My family business had all been sorted and I now had a board of members I trusted with my life and the lives of my family. In the New Year, Joel and I would start travelling to each shop.

We were taking Zane with us. With his accounting background knowledge he would audit the books to see if there was anything amiss. We were starting first with the shop that was doing the best financially, then moving on to the one that wasn't doing as well to compare the two and see if it was the location, staff, management, or a combination of all three.

I knew that Joel worried about me after I had killed my uncle and cousin. But as I explained to him, while my human side was nurturing, my Tiger, well, she's a bitch, especially when her loved ones are threatened.

Joel came driving up the road on the dirt bike they used when they didn't feel like making the hike from the factory to the farmhouse on foot. I stood as he parked up under the trees and walked down the steps to meet him. My heart always felt much lighter once I was held in his arms.

As soon as I reached him, his mouth took mine in a hot, hard kiss that I felt all the way down to my toes. I groaned as I ran my fingers into his hair, holding him tight to me.

When he finally let me up, I sucked in a deep breath of air and licked my lips, smiling up into his dark eyes.

"You good, Sugar," he asked, cupping a big hand to the slight swell of my belly.

"Perfect, honey," I replied.

THE END

The next book is Amy, Sean and Rory's story and is a novella

AMY

Sanctuary Series Book 4

A NOVELLA

By

Michelle Dups

LIST OF CHARACTERS

Macgregor Brothers – Leopard Shifters

Dex – Mated to Reggie – Twins Boys – Ben & James

Falcon

Jett

Duke

Zane

Reggie's Foster Sisters

Jaq, April, Elle

Russo Brothers – Hyena Shifters

Anton

Luca

Landry Siblings – Wild Dog Shifters

Joel – Mated to Julie

Amy – Mated to Rory & Sean Whyte

Jack – Landry Father

Rose – Landry Mother

Julie's Sister

Hannah

Moore Sisters – Elephant – Non-Shifters (CURSED)

Renee

Lottie – Mated to Kyle Whyte

Ava – Twin to Marie

Marie – Twin to Ava

Whyte Family – Multi Shifter Family but mainly Gorilla

Annie – Mother – Gorilla Shifter

John – Father to Kyle (Human) - DECEASED

Kyle (UNABLE TO SHIFT SHOWS SHIFTER TRAITS) – Mated to Lottie Moore

Rory – Twin to Sean - Gorilla Shifter (adopted son of Annie) – Mated to Amy Landry

Sean - Twin to Rory – Gorilla Shifter (adopted son of Annie) – Mated to Amy Landry

AMY

CHAPTER 1

I sat in the back of the Land Cruiser that we'd driven to the airfield in. Rory and Sean were leaning against it waiting for Reggie's sister, Jaq, to arrive with the new plane. Jaq was going to be our new pilot.

I knew my mates were looking forward to seeing her, and even though it was stupid, this was unsettling to me. They were my mates, but recently things had been strained between us. It was my fault. My mates had been as supportive as they could be, which wasn't easy when I wasn't forthcoming about what was bothering me.

In the grand scheme of things, my problem was trivial compared to some, such as the curse that the Moores were living under, or the way that Julie and her sister had been treated by their family.

I just couldn't seem to get my head out of my arse and speak to my mates. As my twin Joel knew, I was great at burying my head in the sand.

The idea of falling pregnant with pups terrified me. While everyone else looked at having pups or cubs as a gift, for me it seemed like a death sentence for my relationship with my mates.

Both Joel and Lottie had tried to speak to me about it and had reassured me that my having pups with Rory and Sean wasn't going to be like it had been with my parents.

But all I remembered was the fights, not enough money to go around, and the constant crying of babies and toddlers. There never seemed to be enough time and because I was the eldest female, I had to help my mother with the younger pups as Joel helped our father keep the farm running. Some of my strongest memories are of finding my mother worn out and sobbing in the garden. We'd just managed to get the pups down to sleep but then she had to pull herself together to start the never-ending washing or preparing of food. Those memories had stayed with me ever since.

Logically I knew it wouldn't be like that now, as we'd completely overhauled the way the ranches and farms worked, but that didn't help.

We were making enough money and I knew my mates would help, as would Annie, Julie and Lottie. I just couldn't seem to get my head to agree with my heart.

I was pulled from my daydream as the plane we were waiting on did a flyover.

SEAN

CHAPTER 2

Leaning up against the vehicle with my brother next to me and our mate sitting behind us, I should have been feeling only contentment, but looking into the setting sun and waiting for Jaq in the new plane, I could feel the tension between us.

Rory and I were at our wit's end with Amy. We weren't sure what was going on with her, as she wouldn't speak to us about whatever it was.

What was more frustrating was that Kyle's mate Lottie knew what was going on but wouldn't break Amy's confidence. All she kept saying was that we needed to get it from Amy. I wondered where we'd go from here. From bits and pieces that we'd put together from those closest to her, it had to do with having pups. It had gotten so bad that as soon as Amy knew she was coming into heat she made up an excuse to leave and spend time in town with the unmated Moore sisters.

The only thing that kept Rory and me from heading to town and tearing the place apart to find her was that Renee phoned us every day and kept us updated. That and the fact that we both knew Amy would be miserable the whole week she was away and would return to us looking pale and thin, with dark circles under her eyes. No matter how much patience we showed, she couldn't seem to open up.

Our mother, Annie, had cautioned that we needed to have patience, and eventually Amy would come round.

What made it so difficult for us was that we'd watched Amy with employees' children on the farm, and she'd known instinctively how to behave with them. She wasn't shy at spending time with the babies, helping out new mothers or just giving mothers a break. It wasn't unusual to see children visiting with her in her office, and she always had small treats for them. All this showed that she'd make a perfect mother but just seemed reluctant to become one.

Rory and I were so confused. It was getting to the stage where we were going to sit Joel down and ask him what was going on. It was either that or tie Amy to the bed and not let her come until she told us. Whatever was happening, it was slowly fracturing our relationship.

Grumbling slightly, I saw Rory looking at me with eyebrows raised. I shrugged and straightened, "I'll tell you later, looks like Jaq is landing."

JAQ

CHAPTER 3

I did a flyover of the main house as Reggie's mate Dex had asked me, and circled the airfield, which was the only strip of tarmac that I'd seen so far. On the way I'd been amazed at the amount of wildlife. Some I didn't recognise but others I did, like the buffalo and the small antelope. I knew from my sister that one of the other farms was a mixed cattle and game ranch.

Using my headset, I let the other passengers know we were coming in for a landing. Not that they wouldn't have known anyway, it was purely by habit. I'd brought three others from my unit with me. We'd mostly been a shifter unit with a few trusted humans in the mix. There had been five males I'd been close to, and they'd considered me their honorary sister. There were the twins' Sean and Rory, next door neighbours of my sister. We hadn't seen them for nearly a year and the three I'd brought with me, Drake, Sam and Jeremiah, or as we called him, Miah.

Drake and Sam were wolves and Miah was full human, although sometimes it seemed as if he was the most feral of all of us. In our unit Drake and Sam had been trackers, while Miah took care of all things communication and computer whiz. Rory and Sean had been the muscle. Obviously, I'd been the transport for drop-offs and extractions.

My only worry was that I hadn't let Dex and Reggie know I was bringing the three males with me.

Hopefully, it won't be a problem.

I brought the plane down smoothly, having seen Sean and Rory off to the side leaning against a 4x4 vehicle. There was a woman in the back of the vehicle, but I didn't think much of that as they always seemed to have women falling over them. I figured that wouldn't have changed, even out here in the middle of nowhere.

Coming to a stop, I started shutting down the plane.

"You need a hand in here?" asked Drake.

I shook my head. "No. If you guys could start offloading and tie down the plane until I know where we'll be storing her, I'll start doing the checks so that she'll be good to go when we need her next."

I heard him speak to the others letting them know I'd be down once I'd done my checks.

They knew how I was about maintenance and checks on my planes.

I finally stepped down from the plane and walked around it to make sure everything was secured. Once I was satisfied, I went to find the guys. They'd already made themselves at home, sitting on their packs waiting for me. They were all laughing and joking, with Rory and Sean looking as content and happy as I'd ever seen them.

Not thinking, I ran up and jumped at Rory and Sean. This was how I'd always greeted them, with an arm going around each of their necks then smacking big kisses to their bald heads.

Out of nowhere I heard a pissed-off female growl and looked up. I saw what at first I thought was a dog, only to realise this one was not domesticated.

The guys moved me off them and went over to the side of the vehicle.

I heard Sean crooning something at the dog and Rory was rubbing her head, but she was having none of it. By now she had drool dripping from her teeth, and I realised I had pissed off a shifter female. I'd touched something that she felt belonged to her, and from the way the guys were touching her I was under the impression they didn't mind her possessiveness one bit.

I felt my eyes get big as my eagle was beginning to realise, we were in trouble. Nothing the guys did was calming the Wild Dog down.

Not waiting around, I took off running with the female hot on my heels. Quickly I managed to strip off and took to the air in my eagle form. As I did so, she just managed to get hold of my tail feathers, which annoyed my eagle no end. In a fit of rage I turned, and with a piercing cry, dive-bombed the dog-like shifter, who by now was angrily raking her back legs over my clothes.

Sean saw me head for the female and shouted a warning at me. I could see his gorilla rising to the surface, as he bent over the smaller female to protect her. I pulled up just in time.

Rory, usually so easy going, was fuming. "Jaq Channing, change back right now. You do not get to attack our mate."

I landed behind the vehicle and changed back, grabbing a shirt one of my team threw to me while we waited for Rory, Sean and their mate to join us.

I hadn't realised they had mated and would have really appreciated a heads up from them. If I'd known, I never would have greeted them like that.

Rory

CHAPTER 4

When I heard the grumble come from Sean's face, I knew that he'd come to the end of his patience with Amy, and somehow we'd be getting the story from her pretty soon. I for one couldn't wait, as whatever it was, it was slowly eroding our relationship. We'd been as patient as we could, but something had to give, although it didn't seem as though our stubborn mate was going to give up without a fight.

The plane came to a full stop and I saw that Jaq was talking to someone. I wondered who it was. I knew she'd want to do all the checks on the plane first, as she'd always been particular about safety.

Seeing the door open, we watched the steps come down and saw three familiar figures appear in the doorway. I couldn't stop the smile that appeared when I saw who it was. Letting out a whoop, Sean and I met the three males at the bottom of the stairs.

The first one to come down the stairs got a back-pounding hug. "Fuck, Miah, it's good to see you," I crowed.

"You too man, but Jesus, I'm human, you idiot. You just about killed me," he laughed.

"Sorry dude," I apologised, still grinning before moving on to the other two, who had been greeting Sean.

Drake and Sam got the same big hug treatment from me. "It's great to see you guys," I said.

"It's great to be here," Drake said, returning the pounding hug.

"Grab your luggage and come and meet our mate," replied Sean.

"You're mated?" queried Drake, looking surprised.

"Yep, come over when you're ready and we'll introduce you."

While they went to get their bags, we went back to Amy who was still sitting in the back of the 4x4.

Looking at her I was once more taken aback at how gorgeous she was in the setting sun, her hair shimmering in the light, bringing out all the different colours that showed her Wild Dog heritage. Her brown eyes sparkled with curiosity as she watched us approach. She smiled and it lit up her entire face. We hadn't seen one of those smiles for weeks. It made me sad that our mate had been so unhappy and we hadn't noticed how much her smile had dimmed.

Reaching her I couldn't stop myself from pulling her into a long kiss. I saw tears shimmer in her eyes before she blinked them away.

She ran her hands over our heads as she liked to do. I'd asked her about it once and she said it was a comfort to her.

Sean took her hand and laid a kiss on the centre of her palm. This caused her breath to hitch slightly, but not in lust as was usually the case with us. Her eyes were still shining with tears.

"Tonight, once we're home, I need to talk to you both," she whispered.

We both nodded at her, as the others came closer.

Holding her hand I said, "Amy, I'd like you to meet a few more members of our unit. They decided to surprise us, and flew over with Jaq. Duke and Sam are Wolf Shifters and Jeremiah is fully human. We call him 'Miah'."

"Pleasure to meet you," smiled Amy, getting chin lifts back from the three males.

Jaq was making her way around the plane checking on the ties and making sure all was secure. Seeing us she began to run before leaping, expecting us to catch her.

We'd forgotten how she used to greet us, with smacking big kisses on our bald heads. We'd also foolishly forgotten the fact that she didn't know we'd mated.

We pushed her off as soon as we heard the feral growl from behind us. Turning I saw that Amy had shifted and was the angriest we'd ever seen her. She was usually a pretty easy going female that went with the flow but today she was so angry that there was drool dripping from her teeth and her lips were drawn back in a vicious snarl.

Sean started crooning something to her, and I had my hand on her, but she wasn't going to let it go. Before we knew it, she was over the side of the vehicle, chasing Jaq who was stripping off while she ran so that she could shift.

Sean and I took off after them and when we got to where Jaq had left her clothes, I saw Amy pee on them. That's when we knew her animal had fully taken over. If Amy had been in control, she would have been mortified at the thought of peeing on someone's clothes while she was shifted. I did find it funny though, as did the males behind me, but I stopped laughing when I saw the pissed-off eagle dive-bombing my mate, screeching as she flew lower.

Sean threw himself over Amy as Jaq narrowly missed them with her talons.

I was furious with her, that she would even think to hurt our mate. "Jaq Channing, change back right now. You do not get to attack our mate."

Amy

CHAPTER 5

Three males walked off the plane, and I smiled as my mates greeted them. We weren't expecting them, but I knew they'd be made welcome once they'd gone through our security checks. I'd gladly welcome anyone who made my mates smile like they were smiling now.

They greeted each other with the same back-pounding slaps that all males seemed to greet each other with, then the newcomers went back to the plane to collect their luggage. My mates came back to me in the back of the vehicle knowing I knew better than to get out to greet strange males.

As they walked towards me with the setting sun behind them, I was once again taken with how gorgeous they were, with their nut-brown skin, strong faces showing their afternoon scruff, and the sun shining like a halo around their heads.

When they got to me Rory pulled me in for a long kiss, a kiss like we hadn't shared in weeks.

My throat grew tight with tears as Sean took my hand and laid a kiss in the centre of my palm.

Enough was enough. I was pulling up my big girl panties and speaking to my males tonight. We couldn't go on like this any longer.

Rubbing my hands over their heads, I leaned forward and said, "Tonight, once we're home, I need to talk to you both."

Getting a nod from both of them, I turned back to meet the males that were approaching.

After being introduced I went back to quietly listening to them chat while I watched the tall, slim female with long, dark brown hair, do a walk around the plane, ensuring everything was secure. I was looking forward to meeting her as I loved Reggie, and I knew she was excited to have one of her sisters live close by.

Then suddenly, I wasn't feeling so charitable about meeting Jaq. She had thrown herself at my males and kissed them. There was no holding my Wild Dog back as I shifted. She took over completely, pushing me to the back of her mind. This didn't happen often, usually only when she felt severely threatened.

She jumped from the back of the vehicle straight at the female that had dared to touch her mates and started chasing her.

My animal only retreated when she felt Sean covering us and heard Rory shouting.

Sensing the threat to her mates was over, I shifted back and heard Rory yelling at the female. "Jaq Channing, change back right now, you do not get to attack our mate."

From under Sean's body, I watched as she flew over to our vehicle and changed back to human, catching a shirt that one of the other males had taken off and thrown to her.

Realising I was laying naked under my mate, I heard Sean grumble as he removed his shirt and pulled it over my head. Running his hands over me to see if I was hurt, Rory pulled me into a hug. I could feel his heart beating hard in his chest.

"Are you okay, baby?" his voice rumbled.

I nodded, feeling tearful as they surrounded me with their warmth and strength.

"I'm good, honey. Sorry I lost it so badly. I wasn't expecting her to hug you like that. I usually have better control."

"Not your fault, love," replied Sean. "We should have thought to let her know we were mated. We were a team for a long time and that is how she usually greets us."

With a short laugh, he grinned down at me wiping away my tears. "I bet she won't do that again. I think you managed to get some of her tail feathers."

I smiled weakly up at the two of them, feeling a little bad for Jaq. It wasn't all her fault. "I'll apologise to her," I said.

"No, you won't," replied Rory, "she should have thought before she jumped at us. Especially as she saw that the others hadn't approached you."

He still sounded mad, so I ran my hand soothingly over his back as they held me tight. I heard a vehicle approaching and knew that it would be my brother and Julie. The others wouldn't be far behind as they were all looking forward to seeing the new plane, and meeting Reggie's sister.

With me tucked securely under their arms we walked back to where the others were standing. Jaq was now completely clothed.

As we got closer the wind changed slightly and blew our scents towards the males waiting with her. The wolves Sam and Deke lifted their noses as they tested the scents in the air.

Their serious faces broke into smiles as they looked at us and dropped the news that would normally make any other shifter ecstatic, but not me.

Grinning at Rory and Sean, Sam said, "Congratulations. You didn't say you were going to be dads."

Even though I knew it would hurt my mates, I couldn't seem to stop the wail that rose out of me. "Noooo, it's too soon. I wasn't in heat. How did this happen?"

In the background, I was aware of the other vehicle stopping. My focus had narrowed down to the look of devastation on my mate's faces as they heard me wail.

I knew they'd think that I didn't want their young, but that wasn't it at all. I just thought that I would have had more time. I couldn't seem to stop crying until out of nowhere, I felt a crack across my face.

In shock, I stood with one hand on my cheek looking into the angry eyes of the bird shifter in front of me. To be fair the slap had stopped me from spiralling and start paying attention to what was going on around me. When I finally took notice, my mates were standing to one side looking devastated, and Julie had Jaq by the throat, holding her up against the side of the vehicle.

Joel passed by them both and came straight to me, pulling me into his arms as I collapsed in tears. I couldn't seem to stop them from flowing.

"It'll be okay Amy, you'll see. This is a beautiful gift you have been given," he crooned, rocking me side to side. As much as I loved my brother I would rather it be my mates comforting me. Again, I thought that I had finally broken us.

"Don't tell me it'll be okay, Joel. What do you know? You're a male, you won't have to carry the litter," I yelled at him.

"Amy, it could only be one pup," he said, still in a reasonable tone of voice.

"I know, Joel, but I'm a Wild Dog. We have multiples. After us, mum went on to three more pregnancies, and they were all triplets and quadruplets. Sean and Rory are twins, we're never going to have any time as mates if I keep pushing out multiples. You know what that does, Joel, you know. Added to that, I wasn't even in heat." I was exasperated that he didn't seem to understand.

There was a pained intake of breath next to me. Turning my head I saw that Julie still had Jaq by the throat, holding her against the side of the 4x4.

The males that had come with her were standing to one side looking uncertain. Clearly, they wanted to help their team member but they were also wary of the big cat that had her by the throat.

Suddenly I felt exhausted. This was enough drama for one day.

"Let her go, Julie, it wasn't all her fault."

Julie snarled and bared her teeth. "Are you sure, Amy? I have no problem keeping her here."

"I'm sure," I said softly. "It's my fault things escalated. I'm going now. I'll see you all tomorrow."

Turning to my mates, who still hadn't moved from where they stood, as far away from me as they could get, I felt my heart crack a little more. This should have been a happy time for us but because I couldn't talk about my worries it had all blown up.

Looking at them, I said quietly, "It's not that I don't want your pups. I do. I have lots to work through and I was going to tell you tonight. I love you both very much. I'm going home, and if you want to listen to my concerns, that's where I will be."

Pulling Sean's shirt off and dropping at his feet, I called up my animal and we left them all at the airfield.

Julie

CHAPTER 6

As Joel and I arrived at the airfield I saw what I assumed was Reggie's sister Jaq pull back and slap Amy across the face. A stranger attacking one of mine? I was out of the vehicle before it stopped and quickly part shifted my hands only. I soon had her by the throat up against the side of the vehicle.

In the background, I saw three strange males, but they weren't my concern at the moment. Joel went to Amy where she stood sobbing, my brothers off to the side looked devastated as they watched their mate cry.

I heard Joel consoling Amy and knew that finally, things had come to a head with those three.

Amy looked at me with tear-drenched, pain-filled eyes and in a weary voice said, "Let her go, Julie, it wasn't all her fault."

"Are you sure Amy? I have no problem keeping her here?" I growled.

"I'm sure," she replied softly. "It's my fault things escalated. I'm going now. I'll see you all tomorrow."

I let go and Jaq dropped to the ground. Amy shifted and took off for home.

Turning to my brothers, I saw they hadn't moved.

In frustration, I snapped at them. "Well, what are you two still doing here? Your mate is hurting, she needs you, and you're just standing here doing nothing. I suggest you pull yourselves together and get your arses home. Talk to your mate, and sort it out tonight, or I'm sending Annie over."

That seemed to jolt them out of their stupor. As they passed me on the way to their vehicle, I grabbed them both by the arm and looked at them seriously before I spoke.

"Amy loves you both very much. Up until now, you've been lucky in your mating and it's mostly been smooth sailing. But don't mess it up at the first obstacle you face. You need to listen to her and her fears, okay. Because to her, they're huge, and you know that we'll all be here to help and support you."

Getting a head tilt from each of them, they dropped kisses on my forehead and left.

Turning to the four newcomers I saw that Jaq was now on her feet.

"I'm not sure who you think you are that you can come here and cause so much chaos. Not only have you upset my brothers and their mate, but you've also brought three strange males with you.

"And I know that they're not expected because I spoke to Reggie this morning, and it was arranged for us to come out and meet you as we're closer. She was only expecting you, Jaq.

"So, on top of all the upset you've caused, you didn't ask permission to bring these males with you. You are one seriously rude female, and for the life of me I can't understand how you can be related to Reggie, who's one of the best females I know." I was still fuming as I said all this.

"They didn't know we were coming?" questioned one of the males. He smelled of wolf.

The human male looked at Jaq in disappointment. "You told us it'd be fine, I assumed you had permission."

Jaq was looking uncomfortable. "I didn't want them to say no."

"JAQ!" There was a wealth of disappointment in the human's voice.

Joel had come to stand next to me in support, his arm firmly around my waist, cupping the slight swell of my stomach, bringing the eyes of the three strange males to us.

I could hear Reggie and Dex's vehicle approaching. I'd leave it up to Dex to sort out the mess that his sister-in-law had created.

Turning to look over my shoulder I saw that the Russos were pulling up behind Dex and Reggie. Getting out of their vehicles their faces grew grim as they took note of the strange males and Jaq standing in front of Joel and me.

Anton came to stand next to me, showing his support, while Luca came to a stop next to Anton.

For a while no one spoke. Dex and Reggie stopped next to Joel. Reggie was silent, disappointment showing on her face as she looked at her sister. Dex was unusually silent as he took in the group of males standing next to Jaq.

Dismissing Jaq, he turned to the males, his leopard showing in his eyes. "Who are you?" he growled.

The wolves in the group of strangers whimpered, showing their necks, even Jaq winced at the alpha waves Dex was emitting. It was hard to ignore the demand to submit, but those of us that were family stood solid next to him, not showing any weakness to the strangers.

The human male with them wasn't affected so stepped forward to explain. "We apologise for showing up uninvited. We didn't realise until about five minutes ago that you had no idea we were coming. Jaq had assured us it was okay and omitted to tell us that she hadn't cleared it with you. We're part of the same team that Rory, Sean and Jaq were in. My name is Jeremiah, and the wolves are Drake and Sam."

Dex looked at Jaq who was looking decidedly uncomfortable under his scrutiny. "Jaq, what do you have to say for yourself?"

To be fair to her, she didn't back down from him, we watched as she pulled her shoulders back to look Dex in the eye.

"It's all my fault. I didn't tell them that I hadn't asked permission. The truth is I need them with me. They're my brothers, and if I'm going to a strange country then I need them there at my back. I also thought it would be good for them to come out here as they've been struggling since leaving the military." She looked and sounded apologetic.

Dex let out a rumbling growl at her explanation.

"You see, the problem we have here is that not only did you not follow shifter protocol and ask permission to bring strangers among us, but you also seem to have upset one of our family members, as well as her pregnant sister-in-law.

"You also didn't consider the security measures we've set up for certain reasons that I won't go into now, nor the fact that we are the protectors for the people in this area, including our Chief and his family.

"We are welcome here only while we continue to protect you. You've arrived with strange males that have not been cleared and now you've put all that in jeopardy," Dex said, looking furious.

Without moving, but raising his voice, he said, "Chief, what would you like us to do in this situation?"

The four in front of us turned, surprise showing on their faces. They hadn't heard the Chief arrive. With him was his armed guard who stood silently around him. Their dark chests were heaving and gleaming with sweat. It seemed they'd run over this way again. The Chief sure liked to give his guards a workout.

Walking closer to the group, the Chief stopped in front of each one as he studied them. Stopping in front of Jaq, his gaze softened slightly as he spoke to her. "You seem to have been the cause of a great deal of turmoil tonight. I hope that you can make it right with everyone. Trust is hard to claw back once broken."

As he spoke to her, a tear made its way down Jaq's cheek.

She nodded. "I'll do my best to make sure I don't break it again. I apologise to you for what I have done, please don't punish my sister's family for my behaviour."

"Ah, but they are your family now, too," he replied, patting her shoulder.

He nodded to Dex and made a motion for his guards to fall in. "I will leave the punishment to you, Dex. Come over this week for a meal and we can discuss the plans for the planes. Bring Reggie with you, and Annie too if you want. I certainly won't complain about having such beauty to look at." He grinned, causing groans from two of the guards, and sniggering from us. Then they left just as quietly as they had arrived.

"What to do with you four?" pondered Dex.

Anton spoke. "Until the security clearances have been made for the three males, we can take them to ours. We don't have any females there."

Dex nodded. "That could work. Now what to do with Jaq," he said, looking at her with narrowed eyes.

Reggie cleared her throat, getting our attention, her face full of disappointment as she looked at her sister.

"Jaq loves to fly whether it be in her shifted form or by plane. I think her punishment should be that she isn't to shift for a month, or fly any of the planes or helicopters. She can go to Annie's and shovel out Lottie's stables for the entire month, while she makes amends to Amy and Julie. They can oversee her punishment."

Jaq's face showed devastation as Reggie laid out her punishment for breaking trust. "Reggie! I'm sorry, okay. I know I screwed up."

"Do you though, Jaq? I was looking forward to having one of my sisters here with me. It's all I've spoken about for the last month. But here you are, and you not only broke my trust, but you also broke the trust of every single person that has welcomed me into their family. I will see you in a month and I suggest you use that month wisely to make amends." Reggie wiped tears from her face as she turned and walked away.

"Joel, can you and Julie drop Jaq at Annie's on your way home?" Dex asked.

Joel nodded. "Of course, Julie would like to see her mum anyway."

From the corner of my eye, I saw Jaq wince as she realised who Annie was.

Luca motioned to Sam, Deke and Miah to bring their bags as he went to where the 4x4 was parked.

"I won't be over tonight, Julie. Please, can you explain to Hannah?" asked Anton.

Wrapping my arms around him in a tight hug, I said, "Of course I will. Don't worry." I let him go and grabbed Joel's hand.

As we walked to our vehicle, I called over my shoulder to Jaq, "Come on, troublemaker. Let's get you to my mum so you can commence your punishment."

Amy

CHAPTER 7

As we took the long trek home, I felt like my whole world had come to an end. My animal was feeling out of sorts after the run in with Jaq and was on high alert. Keeping her on track was exhausting. I just wanted to get home. I didn't want to have to investigate every scent.

Eventually I saw home in the distance. On the veranda I could just make out the figures of two of my oldest friends sitting on the steps waiting for me. Someone must have contacted them and asked them to meet me, knowing I'd need them.

As I slowed to a walk, Lottie stood up, her pregnant belly pushing out in front of her. Renee walked down the stairs to meet me. She had a robe in her hands and wrapped it around me as I shifted back to human. Sobbing, I threw myself into her arms.

"Come on honey, let's get you inside," she said softly, wrapping her arm tight around my shoulder and walking me up the steps.

When I got to the top where Lottie stood waiting for us, I must have looked like a mess of snot and tears, with my hair all over the place.

Lottie didn't speak, but just wrapped her arm around my waist and, held by the two of them, I went into the house.

They ran a shower and helped me clean up, then dressed me in a shirt and panties and tucked me into bed. Then they lay on either side with me tucked between them. Neither said anything but just held me as I cried my heart out. Eventually everything just faded away, as I finally drifted off.

Sean

CHAPTER 8

The shock of how Amy had reacted to Jaq reverberated through Rory and me. The devastation in her voice had been hard to hear, when she'd realised she was pregnant. My heart hurt at the pain in her voice, and the thought that she may not want to carry our young.

Watching as Amy turned away from us, her sense of defeat was obvious, from her drooping shoulders to the tears that I'd seen in her eyes as she turned away from us and ran off. Under any other circumstances we wouldn't have let her go off by herself.

It took Julie angrily snapping at us to pull us out of our heads. Our sister was right. Up until now we'd had a relatively easy mating. Nothing like what some of our family and friends had been through.

Saying goodbye to Julie we climbed into our Landcruiser and left for home.

"Call Lottie and let her know what's happened and ask if she can go and meet Amy, so she won't be alone," I told Rory.

He grabbed his mobile phone from the dashboard and called Lottie, but got Renee instead. She must have been visiting.

He put her on speaker phone so I could listen to him fill her in on events. She agreed that Lottie and her would go over and wait for Amy.

"Rory," she continued, "you and Sean don't need to worry about Amy wanting your young. This isn't about that. This is about her childhood. You need to really listen to her fears. Those of us that grew up with her and Joel get where she's coming from. You both need to be patient. Her mum and dad have arrived, and if it's okay with you, I'm going to let them know what's happened. I think she needs to speak to her mum and see it from her perspective to understand everything."

Rory looked at me, his eyebrows raised in query.

Nodding at him, I answered Renee, "Go ahead and tell them. We just want Amy to be happy."

"Okay," she said, cutting the call.

We continued the hour-long drive home in silence, both of us lost in thought.

When we arrived home, we found Renee, Lottie, and a man who I assumed to be Amy's father on the veranda waiting for us. I thought he must be their father because his resemblance to Joel was uncanny.

Getting out of the vehicle we went up the stairs to meet them. Giving each of the women a kiss on the cheek, I held my hand out to Amy's father.

"I'm Sean, and this is Rory," I said, shaking his hand.

"Jack," he replied, before turning to Rory and offering his hand to him in turn.

"I feel I should apologise to you both, as I know this is mine and Rose's fault. We should have taken more care with Amy and Joel. They took on more responsibilities than they should have at their age," he said. "Rose is in there now with Amy. I'd give her a bit more time before going in."

I sighed, rubbing my hands roughly down my face, scrubbing at the end of the day bristles on my cheeks.

"I think we're all partly to blame for this. Amy is usually so easy going, nothing seems to phase her," I replied.

"We buried our heads in the sand," Rory said. "We're to blame for not pushing the issue sooner. We just kept hoping that she'd talk to us. It shouldn't have been allowed to get this far."

"Here, drink this," Renee said, handing me and Rory cups of strong tea. "I think Rose and Amy are going to be together for a little while, so you may as well get comfortable until she's ready to see you."

Taking the tea, we made ourselves comfortable on the veranda, and waited for our mate to talk things through with her mum.

Amy

CHAPTER 9

I woke up some time later to find my mum sitting on the bed with me, running her fingers through my hair like she used to when I was young.

"Mama, what are you doing here?" I asked.

She sighed deeply, her hand slowing before continuing to run through my hair. I moved over and lay my head on her lap as I used to when I was little, taking comfort from her.

"I've come to apologise to you and your mates, because it's down to your dad and I that you are struggling now. I didn't realise how much our relying on you to help with your brothers and sisters had affected you. You were always so strong and never let on how difficult it was for you. I let you down and failed as your mother."

"You didn't fail me, mama," I whispered. "You were the best mum to all of us. You were just stretched very thin. I tried to help more so that you had more time with the others. We were the oldest, so Joel and I had you and daddy to ourselves for a long time before the others came along.

"It's just that once the babies started coming, we had to help more with them, and it seemed never ending. All I remember is you and daddy fighting about money. I caught you so many times crying in the garden, and you were both so tired all the time. Neither of you ever seemed to have time for yourselves. I remember after one really big fight you packed up the youngest ones and took them to visit Aunty June for three weeks. I didn't think you were going to come back. Then when you did, it was so tense in the house that I ended up spending most of my time at the Moores. I know it got better as the others grew and started helping more, but for me that time is always on replay in my head.

"I'm terrified that when the pups come, Rory, Sean and I will fall apart. The likelihood of me having just one pup is non-existent. I'll always have litters, just like you did." I sat up on the bed and leaned against the headboard next to her.

Grabbing my hands in hers, mum turned to look at me.

"Oh, honey, I wish you'd said something sooner, so I could have put your mind at ease. Yes, we argued about money, but that was because we were not only trying to keep our farm going, but also helping with the Moore's place, as it had basically been abandoned by Frank. All of the families were taking turns to run it and making sure the girls were looked after. Shortly after that Anton and Luca's family died, so we had to add their farm into the roster.

"Basically, we were all running short on patience, and money was tight, stretched between all the farms. But we managed, and then when you kids got older you took over and built it into the amazing enterprise it is now. And that's because you all work together.

"When I went to Aunt June for three weeks it wasn't that I had left your dad and you. You know Aunty June is adopted and is full human. She had an emergency appendectomy and couldn't drive or look after her family. As I was the closest, I volunteered to go. Your dad was angry because I wouldn't wait for him to arrange cover for the farm so we could all go. But it wasn't a good time to leave the farm and he knew that. We were in the midst of planting the new coffee trees, so it wasn't feasible for all of us to leave. He was just being stubborn, which explains the attitude when I got home.

"As for me crying, well sweetheart, I may be a shifter, but I'm still a woman and sometimes you just need to cry and let it all out. Your dad and you kids are the light of my life. So much so that I've really struggled the last few months because none of you need me anymore now you're adults. I'm driving your father crazy with all the new crafts I'm doing just to keep busy.

"I'm thrilled that you and Julie are pregnant and can't wait to meet my grandchildren. Sweetheart, you've nothing to worry about when it comes to these pups. You're in a totally different position to the one we were in. The farms now have a stable income, you have all diversified, and are much stronger as a group than we ever were.

"Also, don't forget that things have improved medically for shifters, with more of us becoming doctors and surgeons. When you decide you're done having pups you can go and see Jett. He'll talk you through all your options.

"Plus, you have two mates, so that's an extra pair of hands right there. And did you really think that between Annie and me you are going to even get your hands on your own children, except maybe to feed them. I plan on being a total pain in the back side. Your mates are going to be sick of me being here, I can promise that," she said.

I threw myself into her arms and she enfolded me tightly. I breathed in her familiar scent, and it settled me down. I finally felt like I could think clearly for the first time in a long time.

"I don't understand how I fell pregnant though, I was over my heat," I said.

She laughed. "Honey, it was fate. It happened because it needed to happen. Nature can be fickle like that sometimes. I hope that you can enjoy the rest of your pregnancy now. Dad and I aren't going anywhere until next July. We'll be away for a month visiting the others in the States and the UK and then we'll be back here to annoy you all."

I grinned back at her, drying my eyes on my t-shirt. "I had better get up and go see what the damage is. I think I heard Rory and Sean coming home earlier."

Mum nodded in agreement. "Go wash your face and you can introduce me to your mates."

Getting up, I went to the bathroom to wash my face, wrinkling my nose at the state of my swollen eyes and matted hair. Grabbing the brush, I went to work and finally put it up into a ponytail. Then I washed my face, although there was nothing I could do about my eyes or puffy cheeks. I shrugged, and grabbed the shorts I'd left hanging on the back of the bathroom door.

Tugging them over my hips and settling them on my waist, I noticed that my waist was slightly thicker than it had been. I struggled to do up the button, and finally gave up, pulling my t-shirt over it. The shirt was long enough to cover the fact that I had left the button undone. I'm not sure how any of us had missed the fact that my boobs and stomach had grown. Just goes to show what you can miss when you bury your head in the sand.

Walking back into the bedroom, mum was sitting on the bed. I took the time to really look at her, and other than the fact that she's only five foot two and I'm closer to five foot seven, it's like looking into a mirror twenty years into the future. Our hair is the same multicolour that both Joel and I have inherited, but whereas facially Joel takes after dad, I look exactly like mum, from the shape of my eyes to the exact same nose.

I never realised how much we looked alike until that moment. It made me wonder what my pups would look like. Finally, I felt a flutter of excitement in my belly at the thought of my children. Straightening my shoulders, I knew it was going to be okay because I would make sure it was. No more ignoring reality. I could handle this, along with my mates and the rest of my family.

I smiled at mum and held out my hand to her.

"Are you ready to meet my mates?" I asked.

"Absolutely. I'm ready," she replied, smiling at me.

Hand in hand, we headed out the door to the veranda where we could hear the faint voices of my mates, my dad and my best friends.

Rory

CHAPTER 10

It was getting late and Amy and her mother still hadn't come out of the house. We knew they were talking because we could hear their faint voices.

Lottie and Renee were curled up together on the couch, Lottie dozing slightly. Kyle was on his way over to collect her soon, so that Renee could go back to her farm.

We'd spent the time getting to know Jack, Amy's father. He was not what I'd been expecting at all. We'd all formed opinions of the couple. When discussed at meetings they come across as flighty and selfish, but the total opposite was true. We found Jack to be a solid male who loved his family and had put them first all his life.

He'd left because his youngest daughter needed her parents, and Joel and Amy had assured them they could cope with the farm. They'd been fine until we had mated Amy, and taken up the time that would have been spent helping Joel.

This didn't leave me with a good feeling. It didn't seem right that we'd been so selfish as to take Amy away from her responsibilities. This had been highlighted when Julie and Joel had mated, and the state of the farm had become apparent. Amy had stepped back up and we'd helped where we could, and the farm was now running as it should be. Joel was less stressed, and our sister was happy.

I wondered what Amy's mother was like. I couldn't imagine that she was as flaky as we'd thought, not with how hardworking and loyal Amy and Joel were. From the short phone conversations I'd had with their sibling Joy in America, I got the impression that she was the same. In fact, all the siblings other than Joy and the youngest sibling Katy, owned and operated their own businesses.

I wasn't left wondering for long what my mate's mother was like as we heard them walking down the passage. Soon they were framed in the door, and it was like looking at Amy in twenty years' time. The only difference between them was their height. I got up and walked over.

"You must be Rory," Rose said, her head tilted to the side, watching me curiously.

"I am. It's a pleasure to meet you," I replied, taking her hand and gently shaking it.

"And you," she replied, with a wide smile.

Returning her smile, I looked at Amy taking in her tear swollen eyes and puffy face. She looked exhausted and deeply sad. Her usually bright brown eyes were dull with unhappiness. Pulling her from her mother, I wrapped her tightly in my arms. Feeling her relax into me I realised how much stress she'd been under. While pressing a kiss to the top of her head, I heard Sean come up behind me, and I released Amy into his arms.

Sean let Amy go when she saw her dad. She went straight into her father's arms with a tearfully whispered, "Daddy, you're here."

"Of course, baby girl. Where else would I be when you need us," he said, gently wiping the tears from her face before wrapping her up in his arms and holding her snug against him. Rose approached, and the three of them embraced, once more a family.

Hearing a vehicle coming up the drive, I turned to see Kyle pull up in his Land Rover and get out.

He bounded up the steps, his eyes searching for Lottie. Seeing her on the couch fast asleep, his face relaxed. Then he noticed Amy in her parents' arms, and his face softened even more. Nodding at Sean and me he stopped by Amy and whispered something to her. She nodded her head and her parents smiled at him. Pressing a kiss to the top of her head he left her and went to the couch to get Lottie.

Picking her up in his arms, he looked at Renee who was now standing, since Lottie was no longer using her as a pillow.

"Where are you staying tonight, Renee?" Kyle asked.

"I will probably just go home," she replied.

"No way, it's too far and it'll take too long. Come home with us and leave early tomorrow morning," he responded.

"Are you sure?" Renee said, looking uncertain.

"Of course, I am. Come on, let's go." Kyle turned to the rest of us.

"See you all sometime this week," he said. "Jack, Rose, it's good to see you back with us. I'll let mum know you're here." With that he walked down the steps with Lottie still fast asleep in his arms.

Renee went to follow but first she spent a long time hugging Amy and whispering to her, before giving Jack and Rose a hug and kiss goodbye.

"Goodnight, boys" she said, patting our arms as she walked by us.

We waited until all we could see was the tail-lights of Kyle and Renee's vehicles before turning to our mate and her parents.

"Well, I think it's time for Rose and I to go back to Joel's," Jack declared, kissing Amy on the cheek. "We'll see you tomorrow, baby girl. Give us a call when you're up, and then we'll come and have a proper visit."

"Okay, dad. I've missed you both. Mum, thanks for setting me straight. I love you." Amy hugged both her parents before stepping back and hugging her arms around herself.

"Love you, baby," her mum replied, patting her daughter gently on the cheek before turning to leave.

She came to a stop before the two of us and surprised us by giving us each a hug. "Look after my baby girl," she whispered to each of us, before going down the stairs to their vehicle.

Jack paused to shake each of our hands. "We're just down the road. Give us a call if you need anything."

Sean and I both nodded and waved as they left. When they were gone, we turned to Amy who was still standing with her arms hugged around herself.

Sean

CHAPTER 11

Our mate was standing hugging her waist tightly with an uncertain look on her face, as the last of our families left our home.

My heart was hurting at the look on her face. It looked as if she expected us to not want her anymore. Yet that was never a possibility, we would always want her. I was sorry at how things had come to a head, but not unhappy that they had. We now had to deal with the situation, but first our mate needed to know that we still loved and cared for her.

Walking up to her, I picked her up and carried her inside, her body tensing and then relaxing, as I laid a kiss on her head. Rory followed us in and went about securing the house for the night.

Taking Amy to our bedroom I lay her on the bed, then stood and stripped down to my boxer shorts. Pulling the covers back I settled on my side of the bed, pulling Amy into me, her silent tears wetting my chest. I had no clue how she had any tears left after the amount she had shed that day.

Rory came in and went straight to the bathroom. I heard the shower come on, but it wasn't long before he was finished and crawling into bed on the other side of Amy. I transferred her over to his arms and went and had my shower. I wasn't sure if we would be discussing anything tonight. Amy seemed worn out and I wondered if it would be wise to push the issue.

Finishing up quickly in the bathroom, I crawled back into bed with Rory and Amy, curling my arm around her waist. I finally relaxed now that we were all together and knew that once we understood where her head was at, we could work through anything.

I was just starting to doze off when Amy started talking. She started with her childhood and how much responsibility she took on for her younger siblings. Then she talked of how scared she was that when we had children our relationship would fall apart with the additional stress, as we were all already so busy and we'd struggle to find time to ourselves as mates. The fact that she would always have multiples added to her stress.

Rory and I could understand that her experiences growing up had affected her greatly. I was a little angry at her parents for having put so much responsibility on Amy and Joel from such a young age.

When I mentioned this, Amy shook her head.

"Don't be angry with them. They were doing the best they could, along with the MacGregors and the Russos, to run all the farms and look after the Moore girls. Frank had basically checked out and left the farm to go to ruin," she explained.

She then went on to tell us the history of all the families and how her parents were the only ones that had survived of the last generation of the four families.

When Dex took over after his parents died, her father had pushed for diversification. Jack, Anton and Dex started regular meetings to brainstorm ideas, and as the next generation grew and came of age, they also went to the meetings. They looked for ideas on how to build up their holdings, so that they never had to scrabble for money as their parents had.

At the same time, Rose was making sure that all the homes were being run properly and all the children were being looked after, as none of them had a living parent to help. It had been Rose that had found a good housekeeper for each home to make sure that there were meals on the tables, and the houses were clean. Other than the housekeeper on the Landry Farm all the others were still the original ones that Rose had found.

She had also been the one to set up the group bank account that each farm paid into monthly. Once a month she was the one who set off to town to buy groceries for all the farms and delivered them and checked that each home was being run satisfactorily.

On top of all this, Rose had also ensured that any youngsters who wanted to go into higher education had been able to do so by helping with applications and going with them to get settled wherever they had chosen to go. She'd been the one they'd called when there was an emergency.

We really hadn't realised how much Jack and Rose had done for everyone.

"That's why nobody blinked an eye when they decided to retire so quickly?" asked Rory.

Amy nodded. "They deserved it. They'd done their bit helping us all grow to responsible adults, so they deserved a break. My youngest sister was ready to go to college and she was the last one they needed to support. We all agreed they should retire, but then things happened. People got mated, Lottie got hurt. Unfortunately, Joel took the brunt of it. I should have seen how he was struggling, but we three had just mated, and that took precedence.

"When my first heat approached, I freaked out and instead of talking to you like an adult I ran away. I broke us," she sobbed into Rory's chest.

The sound hurt my heart.

I knew we couldn't put off talking about this anymore, and with a sigh, I sat looking over at Rory. He nodded. I pulled Amy up into my arms and sat her on my lap. Rory sat next to us braced against the headboard, Amy's legs over his.

I cupped my hands around Amy's face, her eyes still swollen from the tears she'd shed.

"Babe, you haven't broken us. We may be a little dinged, but we're not broken. Yes, you should have told us your fears, but then again, we could have pushed you to tell us.

"Rory and I both knew there was something wrong. But nobody would talk to us about it, they all said we had to ask you. So, now that we know, we can work out a plan to help you feel more comfortable about having our children. There are three of us, so we're already ahead of the game." I grinned at her, getting a small smile in return.

That was a good sign. Even the smallest smile was better than her tears.

"And when you tell us you don't want any more children, we'll sit down with Jett to work out the best way to go about it, okay?" Rory added.

"Okay," Amy replied with a tremulous smile at Rory.

I tilted her head up to mine and pressed one soft kiss to her lips and another to her forehead before passing her over to Rory. He did the same.

"Let's get some sleep. We can hash everything over tomorrow and put plans in place to help you feel more comfortable with everything," I said, laying back down. Amy got comfortable using my chest as a pillow and pulled Rory's arm over her, holding it tight between her breasts.

It had been a long day, but it was the first night in a long time that I went to sleep feeling untroubled.

Amy

CHAPTER 12

The next morning, I woke up still snuggled between my two mates. We hadn't moved all night, and my bladder was crying out for relief. I struggled out from between them and went into the bathroom to do my thing, then jumped in the shower to wash yesterday away.

Going back into the bedroom, I saw they were both still asleep so, after dressing quietly, I went to the kitchen to get a drink. I felt so dehydrated from all the crying.

With a glass of cold orange juice I walked out the back door and sat on the veranda swing.

Although I was tired, it felt better to have everything out in the open. The screen door creaked, and I looked up to see Sean come out with a cup of coffee in his hand.

Picking me up he sat back down, with me on his lap. Sighing in contentment I curled up in his lap, my cheek against his naked chest.

Shortly after, Rory followed him out wearing only a towel and sat with us, pulling my legs over into his lap. He started massaging my feet, making me groan and roll my eyes in ecstasy.

"Babe, unless you want to take this further, you need to stop groaning," muttered Sean, shifting under me.

I felt his length getting harder under me and squirmed a little against him. My body was hot with desire, and I rubbed my thighs together to create a bit of friction, trying to ease the ache between my legs.

It'd been a long time since my males had made love to me. That combined with my excess of hormones, meant my need was off the charts.

"What do you need, baby?" Rory asked, his hands running up the length of my legs from ankle to thigh.

Allowing my legs to drop open, I looked at him through hooded lids.

"For you to make me come," I whispered.

"Fingers or mouth?" he asked, hands snaking under my dress.

"Both," I whimpered.

I felt hands pulling at my panties and before I knew it, they were off.

"Fuck, brother, she is soaked. Here, smell," Rory handed Sean my panties. Lifting them to his nose he took a deep breath and held it, moaning as my scent hit him.

Lifting my chin to him he devoured my lips, and I felt a light breeze as Rory lifted my skirt, his tongue hard and wet working my clit. As his fingers entered me, I screamed as my first orgasm hit me and I felt a gush of come leave my body.

Coming down from that high my body was lifted and lowered on Rory's waiting cock, his towel discarded to the side. I stretched my thighs wide over his hips, settling down, and feeling him deep inside. Sean lifted my dress over my head, my breasts bare, my nipples hard buds in the cool morning air.

I rubbed them against Rory's chest to get some relief, his hands tightened on my hips, stopping my movements. I lay against his chest breathing deeply. He takes my mouth in a hard kiss and I feel Sean's fingers filling me from behind, getting me ready to take him. I shivered in want and need as I waited for him to take me and make me his.

Pressing my face into the crook of Rory's neck I felt my teeth lengthen just as Sean filled me. I couldn't hold back anymore, so I bit down hard, breaking Rory's skin, marking him again as mine. They start to move, pushing into me, filling me to the brim. I felt myself starting to come again.

Letting go of Rory I wrapped my hand around Sean's neck pulling him down to me, I latched my teeth on his neck biting deeply and marking him. I clamped down hard on both cocks making my mates curse as they filled me full of their cum.

I slump against Rory, sated and happy. Sean gently pulls out of me, dropping a kiss to the top of my head. Wrapping the towel gently around me he holds me as Rory gets up. We go into the house to clean up.

We didn't leave the house that day or the next. We made love, reconnected, ate, and talked about a lot of things.

We talked about our plans, what they entailed and how we'd like our family to grow, and what that would look like.

I wished I had done this sooner. My fears all seemed irrelevant now that they were out in the open. I should have trusted my mates. Never again would I keep anything from them.

EPILOGUE

18 years later

We were standing at the airport waiting to say goodbye to our sons. They were on their way to attend university in the UK.

I was a complete mess. I couldn't seem to stop crying. It wasn't as if they didn't have support there if they needed it. We had friends and family waiting to pick them up.

Tucked in between my mates, I watched as our four sons said goodbye to their sisters. I'd been right, we'd had multiples.

My first pregnancy had been our four boys, and yes, it had been hard, but we'd had all the help we needed. My parents moved in for the first four months, and then my single sisters seemed to put us on a rota, because for the first sixteen months of the quads' lives, as soon as one sister left the next one arrived.

I had never felt so grateful for my family as I did that first year.

We'd waited until the quads were four before we had the girls. Having twins after the quads was a breeze. After that my males said no more and went and spoke to Jett. We were content with our six healthy children.

But right now, the first four were breaking my heart by leaving me.

"They'll be fine, babe," Rory rumbled.

I nodded, knowing they would be.

"Don't worry love, we have people that will regularly check on them," Sean muttered.

Rory and Sean straightened as the boys came over to where we were standing.

They each picked me up, hugging and kissing me before moving on to get big-man hugs from their fathers.

From each of them I got a "Love you, mama."

With me in the middle and each of the girls curled into their dads' sides, we watched and waved at the boys until we couldn't see them anymore, as they disappeared into the depths of the airport, to start a new chapter of their lives.

All I could hope was that one day they would want to come back home.

THE END

Acknowledgements

I would like to say a massive thank you to my friend and fellow author Cloe Rowe. Without your encouragement and help this book would never have seen the light of day. One of the best things I have ever done was contact you after reading your first book Redemption Ranch. You have been an inspiration from day one.

To the lovely Jeneveir Evans our early morning chats (well early for me, late nights for you) and suggestions and mentoring have been invaluable. Thank you for taking the time from your busy schedule to help me. Keep that saga going!

My eldest daughter Helen who every day offered positive quotes and comments during this journey. I love you more than the whole world and don't know what I would do without you and your encouragement. Thank you for my beautiful book covers and making me a font just for me. Love you, baby.

To youngest, my lovely Ria, I love your snarky comments when we have to share the same space while I write. Don't ever change. Love you to the moon and back.

To my husband for always encouraging me on whatever crazy idea takes me at the time. Being there for me, always putting me first and for treating me like a queen. After 27 years you are still my inspiration.

To my mum who keeps our house running smoothly I honestly don't know what I would do without you. Love you.

To all my readers who took a chance on me with my first book Wild & Free and for reaching out with positive comments and suggestions.

From the bottom of my heart thank you.

About the Author

I grew up on a cattle farm on the outskirts of a small town in Zambia, in Southern Central Africa. I went to school in South Africa, Zambia and finally finished my schooling in Zimbabwe. I had an amazing childhood filled with fantastic experiences. As a family, we often went on holiday to Lake Kariba and I feel very privileged to have seen Victoria Falls, one of the seven wonders of the world several times.

My grandparents lived on the same farm as my parents and me. It was my grandmother, my Ouma who first introduced me to the romance genre by passing her Mills and Boons on to me, and I was hooked from there.

I now live happily in Jane Austen country in the UK with my family.

Follow me:

Email: michelledups@yahoo.com

https://www.facebook.com/michelle.dups.5/

https://www.instagram.com/author_michelle_dups

www.michelledups.carrd.co

THANK YOU TO MY READERS!

Thank you for taking the time and a chance on me, I hope you enjoy reading my books as much as I enjoy writing them. Books make life a little easier to handle in these strange times.

I write what I like to read and life is hard enough as it is, so there is little angst in my books. They all have a have a happy ending, a strong family vibe with strong alpha males and strong females.

The reason I wrote my first book Wild & Free was that covid hit and I decided that I wanted to start knocking things off my bucket list. As travel was off the cards .... I decided with much encouragement from fellow authors and my family to dust off my notes from the book I started in 1999 while still living in Africa.

I love to hear from my readers so please feel free to message me on any of my social media.

If I could be so cheeky as to ask you to please leave a review, these are truly helpful to indie authors.

BOOKS IN THIS SERIES

Sanctuary Book 1 – Wild and Free (Dex & Reggie)

Sanctuary Book 2 - Angel (Kyle & Lottie)

Sanctuary Book 3 – Julie (Julie & Joel)

Sanctuary Book 4 – Amy a Novella (Amy, Sean and Rory)

Sanctuary Book 5 – Wild Flight (Falcon and Jaq) – TBA

Printed in Great Britain
by Amazon

85758685R00140